for T... Strau...

Playing with Passion

Katrin
Surreen s
Reinhardt
8/2019

A Novel

Playing with Passion

Katrina Reinhardt

iUniverse®

PLAYING WITH PASSION
A NOVEL

iUniverse books may be ordered through booksellers or by contacting:

iUniverse
1663 Liberty Drive
Bloomington, IN 47403
www.iuniverse.com
1-800-Authors (1-800-288-4677)

ISBN: 978-1-5320-4314-7 (sc)
ISBN: 978-1-5320-4313-0 (e)

Library of Congress Control Number: 2018902545

Print information available on the last page.

iUniverse rev. date: 02/24/2018

Acknowledgements

This is a work of fiction. The author is deeply grateful to: The Greater Boston Youth Symphony, the Boston Symphony Orchestra, her cello teacher Leslie Parnas; and, for in depth musical understanding learned from friendships with Michael Steinberg, Leon Kirchner and Curtis Cacioppo.

Prologue

Professor Jacques d'Argenes rubbed his gnarly hands together in anticipation of his office hours.

Today was Elise's day. He loved how she waltzed in and locked the door behind her. Every week, she wanted the same thing: sex. Tomorrow's delight at office hours would be Lily's day of a kinkier kind of sex while she played a Beethoven piano sonata.

There were others who came to other office hours, but most of them came for intellectual enhancement about Beethoven and only occasionally wanted the extra special treatment. One of these ended up pregnant and was dismissed from his class and the office hours as well. She left school for a year.

Five years later, Professor d'Argenes visited a convent to look for a five-year-old child. He was turned away by the nuns for having no business there. Seeking legal advice was something he considered.

Chapter 1

A furious blast of blinding snow and subzero temperatures greeted Yvette as she left her apartment during the 1977 Boston blizzard. She was headed to the majestic Museum of Fine Arts, which was just minutes away. Determined to get to an appointment she'd made just after arriving from Paris, she forced her way down Massachusetts Avenue, past Symphony Hall, and down Huntington Avenue to her destination.

Visibility was close to impossible, but after one tumble into a snowbank, she stood up and forged ahead. After another sliding fall, Yvette grabbed her red leather briefcase, stood up, cursed the bracing wind, and brushed the snow off her long black coat as she attempted to climb the many steps to the museum. Clinging to the railing, she wondered whether anyone would show up for her interview. After a few near slips, she reached the front door. With her heart in her throat, she opened it and shut it quickly behind her.

The guard said, "You sure are a brave one, missy. We almost closed the museum today."

Yvette mumbled that she wasn't sure if she were brave or insane to be out during such weather. Then she quickly walked up more stairs to the Education Department.

Larry Stern, who Yvette had met last week and who was now surrounded by museum faculty members, was engrossed in a pile of papers. He seemed surprised when Yvette walked in.

"Miss Berg! We were sure this storm would have kept you away. Congratulations on getting here at all, much less on time. We had two faculty cancellations, but four of our finest showed up. Please—take your coat off and let me introduce you." With a dramatic gesture, he offered her a chair.

Yvette pulled off her wet red leather gloves and her soaking cashmere coat, hung them on a hook, and placed her briefcase on the table. Her face was expressionless as she prepared herself.

In spite of her thoughtful essay, which they all had in hand, Mr. Stern said he'd like to hear directly from her what she considered her mission to be.

Yvette slid into the assigned chair. Her wet, shiny ringlets of black curls framed a delicate, young—twenty-three-year-old—beautiful face pinched with anxiety. She cleared her throat three times before she began. "I have a degree in viola performance with a minor in music history from the Conservatoire in Paris. My mother is a painter of abstract art. I grew up surrounded by the scent of oil paint and turpentine and the sounds of Mozart and Bach."

"So, you grew up connected more to art than to music?" asked Flora, one of the younger faculty members.

"In a sense, yes, but mother always painted with Bach, Mozart, and Beethoven playing in the background."

The three other adults in the room began to show more interest in Yvette than in their coffee mugs.

"How old were you when you began to spend time with your mother in her workroom?" Donald was leaning halfway across the table with a sharp eye on Yvette.

She was secretly wringing her hands under the table. "I suppose I must have been about two or three."

"As you began to hear more than what was playing in your mother's studio, what music really resonated with you?"

"I began to find the radio stations that had classical music. I was given my own little radio when I was about twelve, and whole worlds of beautiful music were now at my fingertips. I'd lie in my room and become acquainted with the greats like Brahms, Beethoven, Bach, and Tchaikovsky. It became my favorite way to pass the time. Mother was busy, and I was too in love with music to try to be a painter. I discovered at school that I could rent an instrument and have free lessons for one year. I chose the viola since it was quite similar to the human voice."

"By then, had you lost your interest in visual arts?" Larry asked.

Yvette went on to tell her interviewers that of course she'd never lost interest in what her mother was painting or in going to museums. Now that she was growing up, however, she had to do her schoolwork, as well as practice the viola.

2

"When was it that you grew into thinking that music and art were arranged in a separate way, which made you want to connect them?"

"I recently attended an event at the museum in Paris that fueled my desire for the future. There were five excellent lieder and opera singers who'd each chosen one painting to reflect the particular song they wished to sing. It was an experience I'd never expected, and each song—with each chosen painting—invaded my heart, mind, and soul as I'd never felt before. It was then that I decided art students would benefit largely from knowing some of the great old masters to inspire their own works. That is what I hope to do. I think I am looking to create a job where I can work with any age group of art students and introduce them to music that I imagine would enhance their artistic inspiration. With the inspiration of Aeschylus Wagner tried to weave all the arts into his *Ring Cycle*." She warmly looked around at the diverse group in front of her.

They all nodded.

Flora, drowning in colorful scarves, leaned forward and said, "Yvette, this is a daunting task you have set up. Art students are always totally focused on their painting or design or sculpture projects. There is no job described in the museum's directory that comes close to what you see as a job. Why and how would you expect our students to share your enthusiasm—or even take an interest in classical music?"

Yvette moved slightly and her hands gripped the arms of the chair. Hesitantly, she announced that an enormous detour in her studies required her to take a year off and leave Paris. Pursuing this statement, she realized she had to give more details about her shameful past. Her eyes filled with tears. "You see, I was young, naive, and innocent. I became pregnant by a professor who truly had no interest in me or the pregnancy ... he was married with three children." Yvette gulped and swallowed. "I had to take a year off from my conservatoire and go to a convent, known for its excellence in adopting procedures, to see through my pregnancy and deliver the baby in the country. I gave it to a family who had no children and was despairing over their situation. Being as naive and young as I was, this seemed to be the most sensible way to handle a terribly complicated predicament.

"Across the street was a small art school. I visited there often and was invited to sit in on some of their classes. I found many of the students to be intelligent, sensitive, beautiful souls. Their art and spirit captivated me. They soon were close friends, and when we spent time together, they were eager to hear about the music I had been studying. That stimulated

3

my thinking that all the arts are interwoven … connected at a level that is not addressed. Not at my school. Not at their school. We set up days and evenings of fiery discussions, which included why I had allowed myself to get into this agonizing situation. Shall I say, we founded our own independent school." She paused to have some water and smile at her group. "Yes, we added some literature and a touch of philosophy to our gatherings. I discovered that even Sartre and Nietzsche needed to play the piano every day, purely for their own spiritual satisfaction. We held these discussions in students' rooms. While spending hours each week with visual artists, I had time to contemplate the importance of interweaving all of the arts. My viola became an enticing object of interest for most of my friends. Drawing a bow across an open string to get even one decent sound became important to everyone. We all were intrigued by the similarity of doing that and taking a paintbrush to make one beautiful stroke."

Flora asked her if Yvette was as passionate about visual art as she was about music.

Yvette said, "I have been immersed in music for so long … and so intensely. Music has always been on my mind and in my heart. That doesn't mean I wasn't infatuated by many painters. In fact, the visual art students seemed more curious about the world around them. Maybe I should have majored in composition because that is where the truly imaginative musicians were found. The New England Conservatory has set me up to study composition with a fabulous composer who has kindly agreed to take me on. He is known to be deeply knowledgeable about painting and sculpture, as well as music."

Larry Stern, seeing Yvette's discomfort, took over the explanation. "She came here just a week ago to set up a new life, to make her own discoveries, and to try to accomplish this vision she has of stimulating visual artists to be broadened by a love of music. Many, many painters were also musicians: Kandinsky, Klee, Schoenberg, and Berg are just a tiny fraction. Schoenberg put aside musical composition for two years to work on his own paintings. He was a self-taught and much-admired painter. He inspired a younger artist to move into the Schoenberg household to paint there. Incidentally, Mathilde Schoenberg ran off with the young painter and eloped. Anton Webern, a young avant-garde composer and friend of Arnold Schoenberg, intervened to get her to return home. The lives of artists are always colorful."

The group smiled collectively.

"These four artists mentioned were also involved in literature and often torn between music, art, and words. The creative process is a mysterious, elusive part of life. Yvette has a mission. Finding no open route for it in Paris, she decided to come to Boston to see what she could achieve in this hope for integrating, and thereby stimulating, visual artists with the depth of great music."

Donald stretched out in his chair and held his chin up with one hand. His hair was in complete disarray. "Yvette, do you have any idea what art students are really like—and what they really want?"

After sipping from her water, Yvette said, "Oh, I believe they are like good musicians who look for quality in whatever they might be doing. Why do you ask that question?"

"We have seen a lot of students go through this school without accomplishing very much. It upsets me, and I'm sure everyone else here, to see talent not pushed to its potential."

Yvette frowned briefly, her black eyebrows becoming one. "Donald, I also have seen many students in the music world who take none of their work as seriously as they could. I suppose I am reaching out to those who need my kind of stimulation. It may be that this is all a shot in the dark, but I really want to try."

There was more discussion with the other faculty members. Donald and Flora were especially interested, and the interview lasted about an hour.

Larry thanked Yvette for her ideas, energy, and ability to survive getting to the meeting then helped her with her coat.

Yvette gathered her belongings, bowed slightly to her interviewers, and quietly slipped out the door. She headed to the ladies' room to see how she looked. Tears were trickling down her cheeks from relief or fear—she knew not which.

After pulling herself together, she dressed for the difficult six-block walk to her apartment. As she left the building, the snow was blowing from her right side and causing difficulty in progressing the last block home. Yvette trudged on. Arriving at the front of her building, she found it impossible to open the door wide enough to get inside.

After three unsuccessful attempts, a large gloved hand appeared from behind, far above her head, and easily swung the door open.

Once safely inside, she turned to see who had rescued her. Dripping and freezing, both of them looked at each other in amazement at the wonder of nature's force.

Yvette noticed his cello case and his youthful, dangerous appeal. "I can't thank you enough. My name is Yvette, and this is snow that I've never before experienced." Her eyes went from the cello case to the man's big handsome face.

"Well, Yvette, my name is Kolya. When you grow up in Russia, you become used to this sort of stuff. I'm glad I came along when I did." He shifted the bright blue cello case to his other arm. "Are you going up?"

"Yes. The elevator seems to be waiting. What floor do you want?"

"I live in 208, so two floors up."

"Oh! I am in 205. We are neighbors."

They squeezed into the elevator, and on the second floor, she led the way out of the elevator. She said goodbye and thanked him again. Walking purposefully to her apartment, she dismissed any thoughts about the handsome cellist.

∞∞∞ ∾ ∾ ∾ ∞∞∞

Kolya entered his own place and was tempted to walk down to Yvette's to offer her a hot drink or brandy. Knowing it was too soon, he showered and put on warm, dry clothes.

On second thought, he grabbed a bottle of cognac, fixed his wet hair, and sat down to think it over once more. He did not want to frighten Yvette by being aggressive, but he picked up two antique brandy snifters and headed out the door.

When Yvette answered his knock, she encouraged him to come by in the morning to have an espresso with her.

He backed out, feeling a bit ashamed and slightly annoyed, and returned to his apartment.

The next morning Kolya knocked on her door. The smell of coffee wafted through the air.

She invited him in, and he sat on the couch. Gazing at the small espresso cup and pastry sitting next to it, Kolya said, "What brought you to Boston? Paris is the center for all the arts." He carefully sipped the thick coffee.

"What I want to do seemed impossible in Paris. It was so steeped in tradition. I did some homework and decided that I had better possibilities here. I was also running away from a large complication in my life ... I mean skeletons in my closet. You see, I really want to inspire serious art students by immersing them in music of the music masters."

"Music? A-ha! As a cellist in the Boston Symphony, you might be interested in the extra tickets I am given for all concerts. What do you play? What is your background?"

Yvette condensed her speech from the previous day. Kolya looked very serious and questioned the possibility of such a job being possible. She told him they would phone her with their decision soon. Her hopes were not high, she admitted, but she had to start somewhere.

He told her that he would be playing Schoenberg's "Verklarte Nacht" on Friday.

Yvette yelped. "This is a favorite of mine."

Kolya promised to leave a ticket under her door.

They stared at each other. Embarrassment on both sides required a diversion.

He said, "Well, then, until the concert ... and dinner afterward? A bien tot."

Chapter 2

Friday-afternoon concerts at Symphony Hall have one distinctive odor: Miss Clairol hair color (Saturday nights have an entirely different aroma: alcohol). Arriving early on Friday at Symphony Hall, Yvette noted this scent and smiled. Now she had time to climb the stairs and find the seat Kolya had chosen. It was a perfect spot over the orchestra to see all the players and the guest conductor leading a concert she was looking forward to, a concert she needed to uplift her spirits from the recent interview: a Haydn symphony, Schoenberg's "Verklarte Nacht" ("Transfigured Night"), and Beethoven's Sixth (Pastoral) Symphony. The Haydn and Beethoven were almost too familiar, as she'd played them many times in orchestras. But then again, maybe this conductor could raise the music to new heights. The Schoenberg was a treasure that wasn't often done. It is technically a difficult piece. Audiences usually turn away from any program that has Schoenberg on it. However, as time goes by and people's ears become educated, they discover, as Yvette had, often to their own great surprise, that what they couldn't bear twenty years ago is a remarkably fresh, challenging change of pace. And so it was with "Verklarte Nacht."

Yvette leaned on the red velvet railing to look down upon the first violins who were beginning to gather onstage. Now the cellists were entering from the opposite side, and behold! Kolya was holding some glorious dark-varnished, ancient cello and bow in one hand. He handled it with ease, as if it were part of his body, while he chatted with a few other cellists before taking his seat as assistant principal. He looked up, tossed his hair back, saw Yvette, smiled, and then focused on the music. Soon, the conductor walked on to polite applause. He stepped up to the podium and precisely conducted the Haydn. It was a clear, clean—if not innovative—interpretation, transporting her to that world of great music.

Now came the piece she most wanted to hear. There is a version of this for sextet—two violins, two violas, two cellos. She had struggled with it in Paris when she played it with one of her groups. But this later-expanded version for full string orchestra was much richer, and, of course, the players were technically up to anything. The stage was reset for the smaller group, and the string players came back. Kolya looked once more at Yvette, nodding his head as he smiled. The conductor walked onstage more decisively than at first. She thought, *He must take this piece more seriously than the Haydn.*

Pianissimo (pp) is a "supremely quiet" that most conductors cannot achieve. The opening of "Verklarte Nacht" whispered in a pianissimo Yvette had never known any orchestra could produce. Magic. It was pure magic.

The ensuing thirty minutes of intense music, played to perfection, put Yvette into a state she hadn't known for months, maybe years. She simply couldn't listen to Beethoven now. The Schoenberg was a piece she cherished and wanted to *retain* for the entire afternoon, not to be overwhelmed by the Beethoven. During intermission, she raced down the stairs to the backstage door and announced to the guard that she must speak to Kolya Brodsky.

The guard returned with Kolya.

"Kolya! Oh, Kolya! That was simply heaven. I can't listen to *anything* after that. We must talk about it at dinner. What time will you be by?"

They agreed on six o'clock.

Yvette wondered if she should phone the cab driver who brought her from the airport to take them to the restaurant. Pat was so engaging and funny, but Yvette left the possibility open. They could decide together later.

Yvette, choosing not to stay for what most of an audience had come for—after a performance that had awakened and thrilled every nerve in her body—walked dreamily across the street to her home.

She now had time to sit on her couch and read the program notes:

> Schoenberg's genius was such that, while still a relative
> beginner, he was able to refine and develop his own style
> and technique by challenging existing forms and genres.
> Before 1899, when he composed "Verklarte Nacht," he had
> written little music of any significance, and in its mastery
> of large-scale formal design and intensity of melodic and

harmonic expression, this tone-poem was a great leap forward.

We should not overlook the fact that the poem (a touch embarrassing today) that inspired him to write this piece allowed Schoenberg to produce music that is fervent: neither maudlin nor self-indulgent. In the poem, two lovers are walking in a wood. It is winter, nighttime, and the woman apprehensively informs her companion that the child she is carrying was conceived before she met her present lover. The point at which the man begins to reply is unmistakable: a sudden switch to major-key harmony and an expansiveness signifying his understanding, declaring that their love has the power to make the child their own.

Her breathing was heightened by the all-too-familiar references.

Yes, even the program notes were succinct and informative. What a concert. She must go tomorrow night to hear it again. Would the same conductor be able to do as great an interpretation as what she'd heard today? Comparing performances had always intrigued Yvette. She called it her *hobby*. It is, at times, alarming to compare a concert done twice or even three times. There is magical passion in the air or in the conductor's heart that can alter entirely how one piece might vary in its beauty. Whether or not that magic will happen is always a surprise and the reason for a person with a sharp ear to want to hear live music over and over again.

When Kolya knocked on the door, Yvette was no longer pale and drawn. Kolya was elated to hear that the concert had put color in her cheeks and sparkle in her eyes. He glanced at her thick necklace of pearls intertwined with pink crystals—earrings to match—and a pink sweater over a long black skirt. She looked gorgeous.

The couple agreed to speak only French when together.

"Kolya, we haven't even seen each other for five days. I've been here two weeks. How naive could I have been to expect a job? Of course they said no. I really need to talk to you. Going to hear the concert brought me back to life, and that Schoenberg was simply amazing."

As they left the apartment building, Kolya tried to put his arm through Yvette's. She stiffened and moved away even though the snow was interfering with walking.

"Well, you're new to the USA and new to Boston—all faces must be strangers. You're discovering yourself. Indeed, we do need to talk. We hardly know each other." He laughed. "I want to wait until we get to the restaurant and have candles and wine in front of us before I get into serious conversation. Do you understand? Well, of course you do."

They walked through the snow, enjoying the sensation of the mood it provided.

The restaurant was a tiny place hidden in the basement of a South End town house not far from Symphony Hall. As soon as they entered, Kolya was greeted enthusiastically by the owner and seated at a booth for two. They asked the waiter for Kolya's favorite, and a bottle of Montrachet appeared in a silver, ice-filled bucket.

"Well, you do know your wines, Monsieur." Yvette grinned at him. "How is it that you know my language so well?"

"I studied in Paris with a cellist who's a great teacher but not well known. I spent three years working with him and learning French. It was a real adjustment for me to leave Russia and start a life in Paris. I think I can understand, somewhat, you coming to Boston. How old are you, Yvette?"

"I'm twenty-three, but my life has been a little too rich, so twenty-three isn't very young to me."

"Still, you *are* young. I am thirty. I have been in the symphony for three years, and I also feel that life has been too quick and a bit too rich for someone my age. Are you married?"

Her face turned red as she answered, with obvious embarrassment, "I was involved with a married man for a few years. It was an enormous mistake. I think, at times, I'll never recover."

Kolya raised his glass, swirled the glowing white liquid around, and added, "Well, just in case she shows up—which I wouldn't put past her—you should know that Sarah was part of my life for the past two years. She went off to London this year to study art history. She is out of my life now and forever. Enough."

"Can we just talk about the here and now?" Yvette fingered the top of her wineglass until it made a musical sound. Asking Kolya what note that was, he shook his head. Yvette said, "It's a B flat." She grinned after her accomplishment, and Kolya tossed his head back.

"So, we are here to talk musical shop and not personal history," Yvette stated.

"As long as we can enjoy our wine, food, and discussion of Schoenberg."

11

"Agreed. Completely. Now, how were the rehearsals for the Schoenberg? Was your conductor more focused today?"

"Well, it was a bit tricky at first. He wanted that pianissimo to be what the orchestra is not used to producing. We finally did it."

"I have never heard any orchestra whisper a pianissimo the way you all did. It wasn't just great—it was *magic*. Now, did I miss out on anything spectacular in the Beethoven? I am just tired of that piece." Yvette scrutinized his face for a moment and definitely enjoyed what she saw: deep olive skin and curly brown hair just beginning to cover his ears and flopping over his high forehead. Tiny crinkles of amusement at the far corners of his slightly Asian eyes added an exotic touch. But his manner of tossing his head kept Yvette from watching him too carefully. *Does he feel superior? Back to safer territory.*

They talked about music, and Yvette admitted that she needed to know more about contemporary music.

When she told Kolya that she would be studying with Abe Lipinsky, Kolya dropped his fork. "How do you know *him*?"

"I *don't* know him. The conservatory decided that he was the person I needed to study composition and new music with. They set it all up. They were impressed that my great-grandfather, Alban Berg, studied with Schoenberg. Abe, Berg, and Webern were Schoenberg's last important students."

"Good God. I can't believe all of this. You don't need any job. Do you have any idea how lucky you are? When Abe coached us for his Trio, he was remarkably articulate. He gave me, or I should say the cello, an intensely difficult part to pull off. He helped us enormously to make the music sing, chase and follow, spread, sigh, and reach out into some other universe. He is the most amazing intellectual musician in Boston. You will have more than you can possibly do under his direction. He's a demanding teacher. But beware. He seduces, most successfully, every beautiful woman he meets—even at the age of eighty!"

"Passion. Romance. That's why I got into trouble. But you'll agree that I may lead the way in *our* friendship?"

"Agreed."

They toasted to that, both smiling. Then a serious talk about new music took more time and more wine. They enjoyed their veal piccata and noodles. Dessert was a simple homemade panna cotta accompanied by espresso.

The walk home was idyllic. The snow had begun again, and they slid here and there, playfully throwing bits of it at each other and laughing with abandon. Still playful and filled with wine, Yvette invited him to her apartment. He invited her to his. They decided to split one hour into two halves. After all, Kolya commented, he did have rehearsals tomorrow and a concert tomorrow night. Yvette asked him for another ticket, and he said it would be under her door. They decided to have a cognac in Kolya's place.

The kissing. The embracing. The warmth of another body took over. They spent an hour in Kolya's apartment, fully clothed, yearning to get into bed but following Yvette's plan—"no men or sex for a long time"—and it didn't happen. Yvette collected her coat and purse and crept quietly and slowly back to her apartment.

∞∞∞∞∞

No longer did Symphony Hall smell of hair color. It was Saturday. The scent of alcohol filled the halls. Yvette sat in the fifth row under the conductor's feet to watch closely, the guest conductor's style. The Beethoven had truly surprised Yvette. This man knew how to make music. With his magical shaping of the overall phrases, Beethoven's Sixth came to life.

∞∞∞∞∞

The next afternoon, inspired by Kolya's enthusiasm over Abe, Yvette decided to plunge right into her studies with him. If there was not to be a job yet, she wanted musical stimulation.

It was time to call the famous Professor Lipinsky. A bit anxious, she looked up his number and dialed while her hand trembled. Her heart was in her throat, and she hoped Lipinsky would pick up.

"Hello, Professor Lipinsky. This is Yvette Berg, and I was told at the conservatory that you're willing to teach me composition and help me advance my knowledge of contemporary music. Have you been informed by the NEC?"

After a long moment of silence, a deep, raspy but warm and comforting voice answered, "Miss Berg, so nice to hear from you. I have been very much looking forward to this phone call, but I am working right now. I have two hours next week on Wednesday from two o'clock until four

13

o'clock. You have my address I hope. I have one request: I am Abe. Please call me Abe. Can you make this appointment?"

"Oh yes. And I'm pleased to have an appointment so soon. I'll bring some of my scores and manuscript paper. Thank you so much, Abe. Until next week. Au revoir."

⚜ ∾ ∾ ∾ ⚜

Yvette had to collect her papers, scores, and pencils. She also had to mentally prepare herself for serious focus on hard music.

Pat, her cab driver from South Boston, was the first friendly face she'd seen at Logan Airport, and he would be the one to get her there. He was prompt and as polite as he had been upon her arrival from Paris. He helped her into his bumped, scraped taxi. His baseball cap proudly advertised that he was a Red Sox fan. Then, with his wonderfully thick Irish Boston accent, he said, "Well Miss Paris. So, it's been a few weeks now, eh? And how's it goin'?"

"Pat, I am amazed at how many wonderful connections I've made so far. I even live almost next door to a Boston Symphony musician."

"Hey, now dat is really great. I am very happy for you, Miss Paris. Did ya find da wethah' awful? Naw. I think you're one plucky gal. I'll bet nuthin' has gotten in yer way here yet."

Yvette smiled. "But, Pat, I do want a job. I overwhelmed the boss of the Educational Department at the museum and got turned down."

"Naw, Miss Paris. If he was, as ya say, *overwhelmed*, I'll bet he's one dumb-ass."

"We shall see, Pat. Now I have a two-hour lesson with a very famous composer. What is this address?"

"Jeez, he lives in dat ritzy Beacon Hill area. Take a good look at dat and tell me all about it next time we meet. Okay? Heah we are. Good luck."

The exterior of the house was truly beautiful. The windows, surrounded by carefully carved stone, were highlighted by finely polished black-painted shutters on either side. A black wrought iron handrail led up to the newly painted door and highly polished brass fixings.

She rang an ancient brass bell.

The woman who answered the door was an obvious former beauty. Her elegant black-lace dress, wringing hands, and nervous facial movements were the first things Yvette noticed. They shook hands warmly and went up the marvelous curved stairway into a high-ceilinged living room. Beatrice, as she had introduced herself, went to get some tea and called to Abe from the hallway.

Yvette sat on the edge of a melon-colored velvet chair, looking at every detail in the room so she could later describe it to Pat and Kolya. It almost reminded her of her parents' home in Paris: a perfect exterior with a slightly shabby interior that was in need of paint, spiffed-up window casings, and new furniture.

Suddenly, a tall man shuffled into the room. He was brushing back his graying, unkempt hair with a large hand, and his blue eyes were more intense than any Yvette had ever seen. His old corduroys and wrinkled flannel shirt didn't detract from his large, handsome frame and very attractive face.

"Ah. At last I get to meet a relative of a composer I so greatly admire. Let me shake your hand and welcome you to our home."

Yvette stood up.

"Yvette, you look frightened."

"No, Abe." She grinned. "It isn't fear, but I see a wild kind of brilliance in your eyes,"

He smiled mischievously. "Now, is that just plain flattery? At my age, flattery is welcome."

"I always speak the truth. I have a lot to learn from you—beyond all that music history I studied. Everyone who hears your name says you are the best Boston has to offer!"

Beatrice appeared with a silver tray and three ceramic mugs. There was a wonderful touch of Bohemian artistry in the presentation. "Oh. I forgot milk and sugar. Shall I go and get it? Yes, I'll be right back."

"Now, Yvette, where did you learn such perfect English?"

"Well, English was taught throughout my schooling, and it became a goal of mine to speak it well. My father's work brought us to Boston for two years when I was ten. That's where I learned most of my English."

"And what were your emphases in music?"

"I focused on the Romantic composers at the Music Conservatoire. My parents never knew Alban Berg at all. You see, he was never a part of our life. Interestingly, my father took the last name Berg in honor of the wife he loved so deeply.

"Since neither of my parents will ever talk about anything to do with the past, I have to believe what little I have heard. I know that my

15

great-grandfather married but always had a torch burning for Marie the chambermaid and the mother of Albine, Alban's illegitimate daughter. Since he had begun a new life and my own grandmother was never a part of it, I guess that's why I've barely heard Alban Berg's name. I only know what a romantic, handsome, respected composer he is considered to be—and that he was in love with Marie his entire life."

"Do you have brothers and sisters?"

"I have two brothers who showed absolutely no interest in music, but I was driven by it."

"So, you inherited the Berg musical genius?" He grinned again as he slurped his tea. "He really was an intense person and most interesting composer. What got you going into music then?"

"I took a fancy to the viola. I was about eight years old when I started playing it. I still play the viola, and that was how I learned a large part of the repertoire. How many orchestras I played in!" She laughed, beginning to relax. "Finally, I became impatient with all the pieces young orchestras are able to play. When I studied seriously, I discovered Schubert, Beethoven, Mahler, Bruckner, and Schumann—they spoke directly to me. Even then, I felt a yearning to know what direction music took after this period. So, here I am."

Yvette could feel the heat and intensity of Abe's piercing search of her face. She blushed, remembering Kolya's warning, and turned her attention to Beatrice, who was on her way into the living room.

The tea with milk and sugar relaxed everyone's mood.

Beatrice sat next to Abe and quietly spoke of her days as a singer in New York. There was a hint of wistfulness or melancholy in her odd, touching little speech.

Abe pointed to a photograph on the piano and said that Beatrice had been a true beauty with a memorable voice when he met her.

Beatrice either didn't hear him or chose not to acknowledge the 'had been' part.

"Yvette, now we must work. My study is just around the corner. I think we should begin with the Berg piano sonata. Have you studied it?"

She shook her head. "I have tried to listen to it and found it to be a whisper in my ear."

They went into his study, and he locked the door, surprising Yvette with this move.

Abe sat unceremoniously on the piano bench and began the Berg sonata. The piano looked like a scuffed old shoe, but the sounds that came out were burnished and fresh. She listened, entranced. Under Abe's beautifully sculpted fingers, the familiar measures became a study in the propulsive forces of the forceful musical lines. The polish, the surface of his playing, was as battered as the finish on the Steinway, but the power of the music, its tautness and urgency, took her by surprise. It was like standing in the surf with the madness of water churning in all directions.

Berg has probably never been played like this before.

The surf suddenly vanished. Abe had broken off to make a point about some detail of construction—the way the line seemed to be heading one place—but at the last moment, he skipped right over that place and went somewhere else, changing the whole game.

Yvette was fascinated. She'd been expecting what people usually expected when they thought of lessons and learning: knowledge presented in tiny bits, parceled out at a predictable rate for easy processing. This was a headlong plunge.

Abe said, "From Schoenberg, Berg learned one significant principle: variation. Everything must develop out of something else and yet be intrinsically different. The piano sonata is a perfect example of this theory. The whole composition is derived from the work's opening gesture and phrase."

Yvette understood how such deeply informative words would take time to digest.

Abe suggested that Yvette work for the next week on "Verklarte Nacht" since she loved it. It was one of Schoenberg's earliest works, and it would offer her a deep study into the transformation of Romantic music into the new era. "Do you know that Schoenberg was the only person who ever terrified me? Now there was a *truly* brilliant man! If you think my eyes are piercing and brilliant, I can tell you that Schoenberg's eyes were brilliant and piercing to the point of terror."

Yvette was taken aback at this comment, but she was extremely pleased that he had given her such an assignment. She already had the score. She was prepared. When he warned her how complex it was, Yvette said, "Abe, I *know*. I *tried* to play it in Paris with five other string players."

When Abe finally stood up, as abruptly as he'd sat down, she saw the lesson was over. She prepared her words of thanks, but before she could speak, she saw she had been mistaken. The lesson was shifting gears.

Abe was moving toward her with his hand on her lower back. Startled, Yvette turned abruptly, unlocked and opened the door with a forced smile, and said goodbye.

Chapter 3

Abe had misunderstood his new young student, which was rare but not surprising, considering how attractive he'd found her to be. His emotions searching her as they talked had distracted him from his intellectual prowess. His advances toward her were put in abeyance until a later date. What they had discussed about "Verklarte Nacht" had convinced him that she could easily grasp the difficulties of Schoenberg. Yes, he looked forward to working with Yvette.

Slowly and mysteriously, the slush, ice, and snow began to evaporate into Boston's atmosphere. It would reappear as incessant rain when the magic of spring began to breathe its sweetness. For now, the expanse of buildings between Symphony Hall and Boston Harbor took on a warmer look. In the snow and cold, they had seemed a bit bleak, even while maintaining beauty.

Yvette cherished her refreshing walks through the Public Garden and Chinatown. The new discoveries were always uplifting. The food was always delicious and a surprisingly welcome change from her usual French cuisine. Just beyond Chinatown, she window-shopped on the wharves as the harbor splashed fiercely and then gently. She walked down Commonwealth Avenue—with its Parisian touches and elegant homes—Massachusetts Avenue, and Arlington Street. *How could anyone tire of the varied architecture in this nine-block stretch?*

Was it only twelve years ago that she and her family had lived so close to this area? Teenagers' views are not adult, to be sure, but she had never noticed the elegance of the neighborhood. The Bergs had lived in Back Bay, closer to Boston University, and the three Berg children had all gone to private schools. She had been oblivious to the loveliness of the city, distracted by her challenges in speaking the foreign language and going to school where English was all she heard and spoke. Her astute mother had her signed up for viola lessons at the New England Conservatory. Maybe her real musical life had begun right there in Boston, after all.

The fine sound system in her apartment allowed her to dive into great old music while working on the newer composers, which took repeated listening. That was called *work*, and her reward was to melt into Schumann, Schubert, and Schoenberg. Abe had driven her hard on "Verklarte Nacht," but it had paid off. He was proud of her progress.

When he asked why her demeanor and speech were as formal as they were, Yvette said, "When French is how one thinks, the second language sounds altered. Also, my parents were quite formal."

Henryk Berg and Maria Berg had been immigrants in France—one from Germany and the other from Poland—and they had been overly ambitious about fitting in to French society. Perhaps they had been too French for the French.

Parisian society was not openly embracing the foreigners her parents were considered to be. And their last name made adjusting to society more difficult. Even though the boys and Yvette were stellar students, very attractive, and socially more than acceptable, the Bergs felt like outsiders.

Yvette was on the list for society parties because of her kind manner and striking beauty. She loved getting dressed up for the dances—she was a perfect dancing partner—but she felt embarrassed and bored in the midst of the society crowd. *Ah! Society! Worthless conversations about superficial things.* Every now and then, someone who was bright, funny, and a good dancer would engage on a meaningful level with Yvette, but certainly no one she was ever slightly interested in. When she had left Paris and looked over the gorgeous expensive ball gowns she'd hoped to take to Boston, she'd sighed. Memories. Now three months had passed since she'd left with high hopes.

As winter receded into spring, Yvette had still not found a job. Her studies with Abe were proving to be very successful, and she was learning a great deal from him. The only problem was that he glared at her as if she were a juicy, exotic fruit that was waiting to be devoured. Deep down, she knew they were playing cat and mouse. She had to admit that she enjoyed this spice in her life. Abe was turning a bit more aggressive toward her, but she stood her ground pretty well.

Beatrice seemed to be getting used to Yvette's Tuesday visits. She'd warmed up to her husband's newest student and had relaxed a bit around her. She even offered to include Yvette in one of their famous get-togethers.

"A party?" Yvette said.

"Yvette, I really enjoy having Abe's students and friends over here. I am not an inventive cook, but I can assure you that the company will make up for that."

"I am delighted to be included. May I bring a friend?"

"Of course. Our parties are not fancy, but do come and enchant us all with stories of Paris and your life there."

"How many people are you expecting, Beatrice?"

"Oh, let's see, usually about twenty. We don't entertain often now, but we like to make the most of it when we do. It'll be on Sunday evening at seven. Can you make it then?"

"Yes. What shall I bring? I can make a nice pate."

"A pate? Goodness. I have never made one. It would be a welcome hors d'oeuvre. Thank you, Yvette."

Yvette calculated the time difference, called her parents, and filled them in about all this week's activities, joys, and miseries. She always ended their calls with enormous gratitude for making her exciting life possible. She suggested that they visit in early August. It would be a good time for them to see her new city.

Her mother assured her that the new painting, inspired by Yvette, would be ready by then. It was coming along better than she had expected. Yvette had been on her mind the entire time she had worked on it.

The Berg family was not often open with their feelings, but Yvette wept when her mother confessed that she was calling it *Ma Petite Cheri*. Yvette was absorbing a more direct, loving, and honest kind of discourse since she had arrived in the United States. "Oh, Maman. I miss you. Please be sure to tell Papa how much I miss you all. I think I am managing my finances pretty well. Papa has been more than generous! I am having a wonderful time here, and it has been only three months. The New England Conservatory connected me to an amazing composer. He is a fabulous pianist and a man of enormous intelligence. I guess he finds me attractive, but I am trying hard to keep our meetings as professional as possible. A cellist is my closest friend. He plays in the Boston Symphony, so I have free tickets and many opportunities to go to great concerts! I look forward to your visit. Please come in August. *Je vous embrasses de tout mon coeur. Bises!*"

After practicing her viola, Yvette went over to the conservatory for a rehearsal with the Mozart E flat Quartet she had been in for two weeks. Making music was a pleasure after the intellectual strain of her work with Abe and the intense love affair with Kolya.

Sophie was the first violinist of the quartet and deservedly so. She played beautifully and was a hard worker.

Allen was second violin, Yvette was viola, and David was the cellist. It was a congenial group, and they all took the music seriously. They tried to phrase it, pace it in agreement with four different points of view, and synchronize the bowing when possible, but there were jokes here and there during the two-hour rehearsals.

David said, "I think we need to take the opening completely as one … with our bows all on the string before we start."

"But shouldn't Sophie lead us?" Allen asked.

Yvette said, "If we want to play it precisely, there are no leaders and no followers. We have to feel ahead of every note while playing the note together."

"Okay. Let's decide together exactly when we begin."

They worked on the opening for half an hour.

"Wait a minute. Sophie, you are giving too strong an accent to the first note of the second movement."

"Well, can we all accent that first note to show its importance?"

Rehearsals were hard work, but they were extremely important for groups to make music of the black dots on the page.

After two hours, David announced that he had a class to attend, but he truly enjoyed playing in the quartet and thought they were making progress.

They all packed up their instruments and went in different directions.

Yvette could feel Sophie's interest in her and wasn't surprised when Sophie followed her out of the rehearsal room. The strawberry-blonde American beauty invited Yvette to her apartment. Yvette was pleased, and they talked for hours about music, life, and goals.

"I grew up just outside of Boston. Neither of my parents cared about art or music, but I had my ear to the radio every Saturday to listen to opera." Sophie laughed and switched her violin case to her left hand. "I still know nothing about opera, but did I love the sounds I heard on Saturdays! I begged to study violin—lent for free at our public schools—and my parents agreed. Since I was eight years old, I was committed to practicing every day and having good feedback on my work."

They decided to take a walk as they opened up about their musical pasts. The air was soft, the coffee was good, and a bench was waiting for them near Sophie's apartment.

Sophie said, "As time went by, I was good enough for the district orchestra. It was absolutely thrilling to play with good musicians. In high school, I was accepted to the state orchestra, and that was even more exciting. I came from a middle-American family. Music wasn't much on my parents' list of important things, but all my hard work paid off. Meeting new musicians gave me confidence, and we made beautiful music. And then I had an opportunity to audition for the Greater Boston Youth Symphony."

Sophie hugged herself. She was glowing, and a smile covered her face. "Almost all the high school kids were talented beyond anything I'd played with before. I was amazed that I got in, and then they placed me as an assistant concertmaster. We had a fabulous conductor who cemented my total commitment to music."

A bicyclist screeched to a halt and asked what they were discussing.

They both smiled and loudly said, "Music!"

The boy told them he was at the jazz school next door and they promised to attend each other's concerts.

As they headed back to Sophie's place, the sand and slush reminded Yvette of the dreadful blizzard that began her stay in Boston. Yvette said, "Sophie, I'm afraid my path wasn't as direct as yours. In France, there is little freedom in one's choice of repertoire. Players are supposed to fly the French flag in choices of composers. Those of us who preferred German repertoire, both to study and to practice on our instruments, were not looked upon favorably.

"When I got to the Conservatoire, I was considered a renegade for my unusual demands to play the music I wanted and study the German composers I revered. Also, I insisted on dressing in my own style, which people thought was *elitist*. I didn't make many friends, and that is partly why I got into trouble with my Beethoven expert. I thought I was in love with him. Ha! He was simply my path to loving Beethoven." Yvette blushed a deep red.

Sophie asked about what her trouble had been.

Yvette dismissed the question as unimportant, swept the ringlets off her forehead, and flipped her hands downward. Yvette remembered all too well her meetings with Jacques after class: his locking the office door, their sexual variations on the office couch, and his delight in the feeling of her skin. Their short interactions were spent in secret, and it went on for almost two years! Beethoven was still in the forefront, but Jacques's pleasures were surely a close second. She didn't know how many female students were carrying on with him in this manner. When she discovered she was pregnant, she went directly to Jacques after class.

In his usual cool fashion, he said, "This has nothing to do with me. Nothing. I want no part of you from now on—and certainly no part in whatever you do with this fetus."

Yvette had been heartbroken. She was seventeen years old at the time.

Sophie became the addition to Yvette's life that she hadn't realized she'd missed. Kolya was her sole friend. Sophie was able to tell her about the wonderful free concerts at the conservatory.

In her apartment, Sophie rummaged through a pile of papers and found two leaflets. After carefully looking them over, she took a red pen and circled what she thought Yvette should consider. Many were held at the Conservatory's own Jordan Hall, an original wooden performance auditorium with great acoustics.

Life was expanding again in Boston. When Sophie learned that Yvette's mother was a serious painter, she was delighted.

Yvette braced herself and asked Sophie what she thought about her mission.

Sophie grabbed her hand, surprising Yvette, and put it to her cheek.

Yvette quickly pulled it back.

Sophie's face lit up and she asked, "But, Yvette, how would you do that? We are all stuck in our own cubicles—like all the art students."

Yvette launched into the same speech she had given at the museum.

Sophie knit her brow and said, "This is most interesting. Nobody, as far as I know, has been curious about such an endeavor. If there is anything I can do to help you, you must let me know. My own ignorance of art is embarrassing. Do you know what I would give to learn something from the artists themselves? Oh my. This is a very exciting idea. Let's keep talking about it after our rehearsals. What an idea—and so original!"

"Well, Sophie, I'd love to think I was an *original* idea, but to tell the truth, I was inspired by a concert in Paris where opera singers chose a painting and sang an aria to interpret the painting with music. Maybe that's another reason why integrating visual and musical arts hit me so hard. I have a lot to learn. By the way, it is wonderful to be able to talk things over with you."

Sophie announced that she'd been intimidated and attracted to Yvette since they met. She could see the discomfort this caused her friend and left her confession hanging in the air.

Practicing, rehearsals, studying scores, and working with Abe filled most of Yvette's time. Kolya had also been busy with similar activities. He was preparing for a concert with his own quartet. Yvette had been invited to listen to their rehearsals at his apartment. She enjoyed the music. They chose challenging music and discussed at length how to interpret it.

Kolya and Yvette had their own discussions about the pieces. Yvette was relieved that she found his cello playing close to lyrical, technically adept, and beautifully phrased. Respect for this man was essential for their relationship to evolve into something that frightened Yvette: deep love. At times, she thought she had let herself down by falling in love when she had promised herself not to let that happen. Life is always filled with surprises, and when love comes along as naturally as it did for them, she knew to savor it.

After one particularly beautiful concert of a Beethoven overture— Mozart's "Piano Concerto #23" and Rachmaninoff's "Second Symphony"— they had dinner at a restaurant.

The Rachmaninoff had put them both in an intensely romantic mood. Agreeing that the "Second Symphony" was beyond beauty—perhaps the last of the perfect Romantic-Era symphonies—they ordered wine.

Yvette tearfully explained that she'd heard a sixteen-year-old boy make a comment after first hearing of that symphony: "That music reflects the agony of the soul, and it resonates in my heart."

Kolya had a serious expression and said, "So, it takes a young ear and soul to understand Rachmaninoff."

On the walk home, their arms were intertwined.

Kolya leaned down often to kiss Yvette's cheek.

She smiled with pleasure; Rachmaninoff was still overtaking her senses.

When they reached Yvette's apartment, the same essence of romantic aura drew them together. Their clothes dropped to the floor, and their skin sensations were stimulated to desire.

Silence.

Breathing heavily.

Kolya took her mouth and combined it with his own until Yvette murmured that they must get into bed.

"No." Kolya lifted Yvette onto the counter and adjusted her legs so he could enter her.

Yvette instantly came with a loud, ecstatic cry.

Kolya carried her to the bed, finished his pleasure, and gave Yvette more ecstatic moments.

Drenched in sweat, they clung to each other and kissed deeply.

∞∞∞∞∞

Tuesday was Abe day, and Yvette asked about his marriage.

"Yvette, I met Beatrice fifty years ago. I was young, she was five years older than I and recently divorced. She fell in love with me at first sight. Yes, it was embarrassing. I was not an experienced man. Things escalated quickly. I didn't even know what was happening until we were married, had her young boy to raise, and were living in California. Schoenberg was my teacher, and I was teaching at the university. Beatrice was ecstatically happy to be with me—to be as far from her ex-husband as possible—and when she became pregnant, well, you can imagine. Our son was thrilled as well at the thought of a new baby."

"Abe, were you honestly happy in your situation?"

"I was consumed with composing. That was my happiness. The problems with Beatrice were beginning to creep out of corners here and there. Our son started to show signs of trouble in school, sending Beatrice into tirades that frightened me. She had initially been agreeable, but as time went by and our baby was closer to being born, she began to appear slightly crazed. Once our boy was born, things calmed down. Yvette, when I say she was madly in love with me, it is not that I am boasting. She was willing to put up with all of my peculiarities. Did I love her? I'd have to say that I did, but then, what did I know about love? You know firsthand about my desire for beauty, and she was a true beauty. Her ability to run a household was something of a larger challenge than we expected, but we managed. I should say *she* managed."

"Did she behave lovingly toward you ... if not the children?"

"Yes. She was a loving wife—until she realized there were mutual attractions between a few other women and me. That made her furious.

25

But, again, she coped. When she became pregnant with our second child, I was afraid she was really heading for a breakdown. It didn't happen, and her thrill at having another baby was her complete focus. We were still in California, socializing with your great-grandfather, Schoenberg, and many musicians. Our family enjoyed all of that. Her parents had been, and continued to be, unusually generous financially. That was important to ease the pressure on our marriage. Beatrice felt free of worry about finances.

"So, now we had two boys, and then came Lily. What a gorgeous baby she was! We must have been annoying to all our acquaintances as we showed off this baby beauty on any possible occasion."

"Did this make Beatrice any happier? Was she kinder to all the children then?"

"Surprisingly, no. She was slowly evolving into an impatient woman whose looks were declining with every tirade she had. She had tirades over the most unimportant things. I was no good as a father at that point. I think I was never a good father. The children needed at least one reliable parent, and they had none … an effect that has, sadly, only grown worse as the years go by. Beatrice tried to keep up her cello playing on a small scale. I tried to help her by writing little pieces for her to work on. We muddled through ten years in California, and then I was offered a job at Harvard. It seemed like a great opportunity at the time, but in retrospect, it was a bad decision to go to a university where new music is not appreciated and rarely played. I had great friends, composers, in California, people who nurtured my talents. At Harvard, it was all infighting and ugly. Some of my composition students were talented—some were *very* talented—but I missed the close and deep relationships with my friends in California."

"So, you have had to make big adjustments over the years?"

He laughed long and hard, and in a raspy voice, he said, "Yvette, you could never imagine how many changes and difficulties have been in my life. This is not for you to mess your mind with. You have enough decisions and questions to answer for a twenty-three-year-old."

◆◆◆ ∞ ∞ ∞ ◆◆◆

Yvette had found all the necessary ingredients for her pate, doubling the recipe to be sure there was enough. She called Pat, and his voice gave away his joy at hearing from her. She asked him to take her and a friend to Abe's party.

"A friend? Hey, c'mon, Miss Paris. Is this a friend or some new lover? I gotta know how to greet 'em. Sure. I'll be there at seven. You can always count on ole Pat!"

Yvette took care in dressing well that evening. She loosened all the curls so they surrounded her face and hung down softly onto a light blue sweater. Then a scarf from France with hints of blue and purple went around her neck, tied in the back. Small blue crystal earrings completed the outfit.

When Kolya arrived, Yvette asked him why he looked anxious.

"You know I played Abe's Trio. He is a frightening man. His coaching sessions were beyond intense. He is ruthless and demanding. It is not clear that we ever met his expectations, though he never came to the concert when we played it. Naturally, I am anxious about seeing him."

"Cheri, here is what we will do. To distract you momentarily, we speak only French until we get to the party. Once there, you will find at least twenty musicians to talk to—musicians you probably have never met. And you will avoid Abe. I can flirt superficially to keep him away from you."

Pat arrived early. The air was cool and refreshing without being cold.

Yvette held onto her pate while Pat opened the cab door for them, shook Kolya's hand graciously, and told Miss Paris that she had good taste in friends. "And ya betta' hold onto dat huge bowl ya got there—sure smells awful good." He knew just where they were going and allowed them to speak French with no interruptions. As they paid him, Yvette said that they would walk home.

They climbed the steps, and Kolya held onto the railing.

Beatrice answered the door with a half-hearted smile and motioned that they should go upstairs.

The sounds of laughter and chatter filled the air.

As they reached the living room and used the standing coat hanger, Abe charged over and engulfed Yvette so that she disappeared in his embrace.

"My little beauty. What? Is this your date for tonight? But I know Kolya's playing very well if I don't know him at all. He played my Piano Trio. Welcome!"

Yvette handed the pate to someone in an apron.

27

Kolya smiled, nodded at Abe, and spotted the bar. He couldn't get there quickly enough. After ordering a double scotch on the rocks, he surveyed the room. He knew no one there. He sat down in a deep chair and looked at all the beautiful women, the paintings, and the room. The guests included famous musicians who Kolya only knew from CD covers.

A woman walked over and sat on the floor next to him. They engaged in a lively conversation, and at last he no longer felt anxious. He kept his eye on Yvette, and Abe often had his hand on the small of her back.

Beatrice fluttered around as an almost invisible hostess, keeping her eye on no one in particular. She seemed all too familiar with her husband's various attractions to other women.

Music publishers clustered together and talked shop. Musicians found each other and discussed various concerts, pieces of music they were working on, and the dreadful winters in Boston. A few people were discussing the books they were reading. The pate was commented on by many; Beatrice reaped the rewards and compliments on it.

∞∞∞ ∽ ∽ ∽ ∞∞∞

Abe stood with three people and introduced his new student. She recognized each one from her CD of his piece. They had commissioned his now-famous Second Piano Trio.

He announced that if anyone wanted to hear his piece done truly beautifully, the musicians were here.

Kolya frowned, walked over, and pulled Yvette away.

"You're not insulted, I hope!" Abe said.

"No, not insulted. But damn it, Abe, we played that piece, loving every note. It went very well, in fact. Your coaching was essential to our success. It was appreciated by the audience, but it would have been even more appreciated if they'd seen you at our concert."

Yvette said, "Oh, yes, Abe. I do want to work with you on the Trio. I have the recording, but I need the score."

"No problem. I'll get that right away before I forget."

"Yvette, I really want to leave as soon as you get the score. I hate to drag you away, but I need to go. We've been here long enough."

"Beatrice, I will pick up the bowl on Tuesday. Abe, you are expecting me on Tuesday?"

He answered that it was his favorite day of the week.

They walked down the circular stairway to the beauty of Beacon Hill. Gas lamps lit the way over the brick sidewalks.

"At least it's not snowing. Kolya, for the first time since I met you, you are in a frightful mood. Did you feel insulted by him?"

"Not insulted. No. I think a better word would be *outraged* at his dismissive attitude about our herculean efforts working on his piece and his usual seductive way toward you. It's obvious to me that this flirtation has gone both ways. Are you having an affair with him? Beatrice has become so used to it that she ignores him when he is so obviously infatuated."

Yvette felt his fury and understood it, but she didn't know what to say.

They walked in silence along her favorite path through the Public Garden and then down those nine blocks.

As they took the elevator to the second floor, they remained silent.

Kolya wanted to get something from his apartment. After he opened his door, he shut it as quickly as he'd opened it. He whispered to Yvette that Sarah was in his apartment. She was in the past and was supposed to be in England, and he was terribly embarrassed. He turned the gasping Yvette toward her apartment and said he'd return when he had finished taking care of this large interruption.

Rushing to her apartment, she stood in front of the full-length mirror and gave herself a talking-to.

Yvette, you promised yourself three months ago not to fall in love. See where this leads you? More torture and agony. No champagne to toast to anything now. What if he falls back in love with this girl? I can't even think straight.

She found her phone and called Sophie who insisted that she walk over there right away. It was still early enough to be safe. Red-eyed Yvette threw on her coat, put the keys in her pocket, and walked as if in a drunken state to Sophie's.

"You look ghastly, Yvette. Take off everything, and I will run a bath for you. We will talk later about what happened, but for now, I'm giving you a glass of wine and a hot bath."

Soaking in the warmth up to her chin was utterly relaxing. It didn't seem odd when Sophie began to rub her body with water. It felt too good.

Sophie pulled a big towel from somewhere and told Yvette to stand up. She covered her with the towel and walked her over to the couch. Yvette was in a trance as she lay down on her back. Sophie tip-toed to the bathroom and returned with a bottle of lotion. Slowly pulling the towel back, in silence, she began to massage Yvette's naked skin. Her neck. Her shoulders. She slowly caressed Yvette's breasts with the lotion. Then down to her stomach.

Yvette uttered quiet groans of pleasure.

Sophie put her mouth on Yvette's upper thighs until her tongue was between Yvette's legs.

Yvette was moaning, encouraging Sophie to stay right there. Her body convulsed with sexual ecstasy again and again. Then she drifted into sleep, unaware of the softness of another body on top of hers. It was a completely new experience for Yvette, yet she was not even conscious of it since she was very upset with Kolya and completely confused when Sophie put her in the bathtub.

Chapter 4

Sophie spent some minutes convincing Yvette that she was not a lesbian and that she had been overcome with a new desire when Yvette looked so beautiful in the bath.

Yvette, embarrassed, told Sophie that it was her first experience being naked with a woman. "Let's leave it at that, Sophie. It happened, it's over, and I thank you for rescuing me."

Both girls dressed quickly.

The ringing phone stabbed the air into thin slices of metal throughout Sophie's apartment.

Sophie picked it up. "Hello? Yes, she's here. One minute please."

"Oui. Yvette. How did you find me here?"

"I went into your apartment, desperate to talk to you, picked up your phone, and pressed redial. It was the only thing I could think of to do. Yvette, we have to meet at noontime today at Au Bon Pain. I have rehearsals from ten till noon and then one thirty until four. I must speak with you. Will you meet me?"

"Yes, at noon," Yvette whispered. Then she turned to Sophie looking blank, her hands open and up, as if surrendering to she knew not what.

"Yvette, sit down and tell me what happened last night."

Yvette told her about Abe's party, Kolya and their relationship, which Sophie had known nothing about till now, and the shock of finding his ex-girlfriend—who was supposed to be in London until the summer—in his apartment when they returned. Sophie suggested that they walk over to Yvette's apartment, have some coffee, and do whatever it took to cheer her up.

It was Monday morning, and students were going here and there with instruments and without instruments. People were parking their cars in front of Symphony Hall to buy concert tickets. The air was refreshing, even if a cloud covered sky got in the way. The walk to Yvette's took about ten minutes.

They decided to buy a few things for Yvette's apartment after Sophie had seen it. Shopping was not something Yvette enjoyed, but it was bearable doing a chore with a friend. A friend was actually something new for Yvette—except when she had made friends with all the art students in the countryside of France. She decided it was time, soon, to tell Sophie everything. She would begin when she had made coffee in her apartment.

They picked up two croissants and went up to number 208.

"Yvette, this is an acceptable place. How'd you find it?"

"I wrote to the New England Conservatory about studying part-time there, and I asked them to find me a good place to live. Oh, Sophie, I promised myself not to get involved with any man, but before I knew it, I had fallen for Kolya. He lives two doors down from me. Remember that horrid day of the blizzard? He rescued me when I could not open the door to the apartment building. The next morning, we had coffee at my place, and I discovered that he had a girlfriend who was studying art in London for a year. Truly. That's all I knew. I didn't ask any questions because we were having such a wonderful time discussing concerts and picking apart his rehearsals with his quartet. They play in his apartment, and I go as often as I can."

"Lucky you. Things certainly fell into place."

"Yes. I guess that's true, Sophie. I finally gave in, and we started having wonderful sex. He has a passionate Russian heart and soul and a strong sexual drive. He's smart and wise, kind and sweet to me. I think of him as my Russian bear. This was the first horrid interruption in our pleasant two-month relationship. I have no idea where it's going, especially now, but I think I love him … and I know he loves me."

The coffee was gurgling in the tiny espresso pot and filling the room with its wonderful aroma.

"But that was quite a shocking interruption!" Sophie said.

"A little too shocking, but I have been through so many 'too-shocking' experiences for my twenty-three years that I should be stronger than I am. Do you want sugar or jam with our croissants?"

After finishing breakfast, they looked around the apartment, each having a few ideas of how to perk it up. Sophie knew just where to go to find the charming additions.

They walked to Newbury Street and discovered delightful little shops where they found a small blue and white Chinese vase, a hanging paper lamp, and some dried flowers in inspirational colors. Saving the wall space for Maria Berg's paintings, they turned down the idea of posters. The apartment had come equipped with perfectly serviceable china, but Yvette fell in love with some antique wineglasses. They were delicate, and etched flowers swirled around the glass and down the stems. Intimidation of even touching them overcame both girls.

"These are exquisite! Were they made by an angel?" Sophie asked.

The owner replied, "Ya know, they might've been! No, they're from the 1800s. From France, in fact."

It was a deal Yvette couldn't resist. The price was good since there were only five left. They found pale blue espresso cups and a small flowered tray for the coffee table. They could display the wineglasses and cocktail napkins.

On the way back, they bought fresh daffodils, a shell-colored small blanket to throw over the back of the sofa/bed, and a few small multicolored pillows for the sofa. Their tastes were not exactly the same, but they were cheerful with their choices of the things to uplift Yvette's surroundings.

When Sophie asked if it all was affordable, Yvette said that her father was generous. He had set her up financially so that she didn't have to worry about that part of her life.

Sophie pouted at the realization that Yvette was rich and she was not. A large pause preceded a dark mood.

While walking back to Yvette's apartment with the huge bags, which weren't too heavy, Yvette began to respond to Sophie's curiosity about her life. Yvette wasn't thrilled to divulge her secrets. They stopped for more coffee and pastries to divert the conversation, and Yvette said that she would open up about her past life at some other time.

Sophie shrugged.

Back at the apartment, distracted by the lovely and lively purchases, the black mood melted. They chatted about simple things as they hung the paper lamp and put out all the lovely purchases. They transformed the tiny, dull apartment with an array of warm colors and delicacy that perfectly reflected Yvette. She quickly showered and changed her clothes. She'd been strongly urged to buy some Gap jeans, which fit her like a glove.

After putting on bit of makeup, she went down to meet Kolya at Au

Bon Pain. Yvette instantly spotted him at a table close to the wide glass door. He looked dark and stormy, as if he were in pain.

"Yvette, my darling girl. I am so, so terribly sorry. I can't apologize enough to you. I've ordered soup and a sandwich for us both. We only have a short time to go into a long conversation. An explanation will have to wait till tonight. Will you be free?"

"Yes, and I need to have a real talk with you. We have had such fun, but we have not gotten to know each other on a serious level. I think I still love you, Kolya."

"And I know I love you, especially in jeans."

His smile melted her heart. "Well, Sophie convinced me that I have to wear jeans if I live in America. We bought them today. I actually like them!" She smiled back, almost happily.

As their food arrived, Kolya told her they were rehearsing the Beethoven Triple Concerto with a good cellist, which was the most difficult part, a good pianist, and a decent violinist. He promised to leave tickets for Friday and Saturday under her door. Also on the program was a symphony by Sibelius and a Mozart overture. Yvette had to know which Sibelius. *Oh, heavens*, she thought, *another fabulous concert.* Sarah was not even mentioned. That would wait till tonight. "Will we be able to be alone when we talk?"

"Of course we'll be alone."

"Well, you have to come to my place tonight and see what I did this morning. I'll cook for us."

They finished lunch on a surprisingly upbeat note, stood up, hugged each other, and went in opposite directions.

Yvette thought about her lesson with Abe tomorrow. *He will understand that I am not prepared in my usual way. Most important right now is to straighten out Kolya and me. Off to the grocery store to choose something easy to make for dinner since I must take a nap. I guess they can deliver a case of wine. I'll get some Chardonnay, some Amarone, and a bottle or two of Chianti. My new glasses will be so heavenly. Tonight might be fun. We shall see.*

Kolya knocked on the door, which was a surprise. Yvette let him in, and he handed her a bottle of wine. She asked him to speak French with her.

"Yvette, you've added some lovely things here. They are charming and elegant." He pulled the reading chair over near the couch where there was an open bottle of wine. With his elbows on his knees and his chin

34

cupped by his large hands, he looked adorable. His clean white turtleneck was tucked into his burgundy corduroys. The outfit showed off his broad-shouldered, masculine body. He was her Russian bear. "These glasses are really something. Where did you ever find them?"

"Sophie took me down to Newbury Street. I adore them, especially on the new tray. Have some cheese and wine. Then I want to hear your life story, in an abbreviated version, from Russia until joining the Boston Symphony." In her jeans and black sweater, she looked like an artist curled up on the couch.

His hair was still damp, curly, and messy from the shower. "No, Yvette. I first want to tell you about Sarah and me and what happened last night. You see, she was supposed to be gone for a year, studying art history in London. When she hadn't heard from me in a month, she decided to come back for a visit to check on me and her family. As I told you before, we had been seeing each other for almost a year. She had a key to my place, and I have one to hers, though it's rented out until the fall." He stood up and started pacing, touching the paper lamp and the lively daffodils.

"Well, as soon as she saw you with me, she instantly figured it all out. She is very sharp but has no deep feelings. She knew that I'd meet someone else if she left Boston for so long. When I told her that you and I were very close—that I had no intention of spending time with her anymore—she remained dry-eyed and a bit stiff. Can you believe this part? She bought a one-way ticket back here. She told me about her life in London, her work, and that she had been dating an older man for a few months. It was a remarkably decent conversation, considering what a shock it had been to find her there. It took some time to convince her that a one-way ticket was ridiculous because I had no more feelings for her at all. She left after an hour and took the few belongings she'd left in a drawer in my place." Kolya sat down next to Yvette.

Yvette took note of how serious he'd become. Their relationship had veered in a new direction in just twenty minutes. He asked her to tell him about her past.

"My past?" Yvette reflected and articulated parts of a long story. She sat up in a professional manner. "Being Jewish in Paris is not the easiest position to be in. Prejudice still runs deep in that society. People in the arts are much more open-minded than the general public. But being stubborn about what music I wanted to play and study was not what professors wanted or liked. I was a pariah until I took a course on Beethoven. I'd go to after-class sessions to know more. Falling in love with Beethoven was what it was all about. But the teacher wanted everyone to fall in love with him—Jacques d'Argenes. Needless to say—no details now—there was a pregnancy, which he wanted absolutely no part of. My Jewish parents thought an abortion was the right thing, but I foolishly insisted on giving up a treasure for adoption. Do you understand why I would not have an abortion? There are many childless middle-aged couples who are dying for a child. I had the baby at a convent, suffering miserably, and I was unable to speak for days until I heard about the adopting family. It was great news. That's it for now."

Kolya warned her, almost threateningly, that she would want to know about the baby later in her life.

Yvette frowned dismissively, tossing her hand off to the side. Deep down, she was terrified. "I went back to school with new ideas of incorporating music into art schools. It became something close to an obsession. I had no interest in boyfriends or romance for two years, but when I met you, I knew I was heading for trouble. Somehow it doesn't feel like trouble. We've had so much fun, and I am on good birth control pills. Enough! Let's just eat."

She stood up, casually walked over to the kitchen, and pulled a crispy-skinned, roasted-garlic chicken out of the oven. She took a salad out of the refrigerator. It had many different greens, tiny tomatoes carefully placed around the edge of the platter, and at least three different cheeses crumbled into fragments on top. With a fresh baguette, it was a perfect dinner.

Kolya helped her move it to the table. The daffodils, bursting with color in their blue and white vase, provided a cheerful ambience. As always, Yvette had at least six candles glowing. They sat down, still not having touched each other. Yvette told him that dessert was embarrassingly simple: vanilla ice cream doused with Chateau d'Yquem.

"Isn't it amazing that we have had this marvelous time together without either of us cooking for each other!" Kolya remarked. There was a softer, more tender tone in his voice. His face looked almost radiant.

Yvette was pleased. "Finding good restaurants has been a treat for me. We've had some fabulous dinners out, for which I really am grateful to you. I am more than happy to have a chance to cook for you, Kolya. It's about time." Yvette's face reflected his radiance.

They relaxed and enjoyed every bite of her excellent cooking. The baguette perfectly absorbed the juices of the chicken.

"Garlic chicken has never tasted like this. I detect a bit of butter?"

"My mother is a fabulous cook. I cooked the chicken the way I remember her doing it. I spent many hours with her in the kitchen. I was always watching her and talking with her. Maman is a special person. I love her very much. I can't say the same exactly about my father. He is colder and more distant, but Maman insists that he is perfect for her and to her. I have to believe it since she is a content, happy person. Just wait till you see her paintings. Are you enjoying these glasses?"

"The food is so good. I have neglected to tell you how the glass enhances the wine. What is this wine?"

"It is one of the Chardonnays I bought today. I chose a case of a variety of wines and had it delivered. Now I am prepared for the next twelve nights! If we eat meat, I will bring out my beloved Amarone for us to enjoy. I can plan to cook for us for twelve nights, Kolya."

"Yvette, where do you see our relationship going?"

Her face became serious. She finished her mouthful of chicken before answering him.

"I haven't had to give it much thought. I've been having too much fun. I believe that we are as in love with music as any two people could be. It has been the main force that has drawn us together. It's all we have done except making love, which, by the way, has been beautiful and satisfying. I am no expert, but it seems that you are a great lover, Kolya."

"I make love only when there is love to respond to. I have had sex before with many women, but I have never been able to make love the way you and I have. Can a relationship survive only on music and sex and food?"

"Who can see the future? When two people establish a companionship based on those three most important things—and they feel love and attraction for each other—I'd say it's a very important start. In fact, I'd say it is the most important start. In my view, a great couple is always starting over again. Every single day is to be cherished—even if there are bumps along the way."

"Then you're saying that we really do have something special?"

"I have never felt this way with anyone before you. Are you asking if it will last? I will say again—we can't see the future."

"Don't you think we need to explore life beyond those three things?" Kolya asked.

"Of course I do! But we've known each other a short time. We have museums, lakes, oceans, woods, and books to explore together. We have time! We are both young and very involved in our work. There will be time, soon, to do these other explorations. I have to show you my Paris. You have to take me to your Russian world so I can meet your parents and understand how you came to be who you are. Yes. We have so much life ahead of us. Do you see spending that time with me?"

"I do, Yvette. You are the second true love in my life. Sarah was no love, but before her, I loved Natalie. I really loved her. But that's for another time."

"Do you know how much the cello seems to be a simple extension of your gorgeous body? When you walk onstage at Symphony Hall, you and your cello are one being. I can't say the same at all for me since the viola is a much smaller part of my life. Having studied music history—and now composition—with Abe, there is more brainwork required. I am only beginning to understand the enormous gulf ... gap ... between knowing the history of music and knowing the complexities of how it evolves and gets made. Since music is truly the most abstract form of art, it requires great amounts of time to absorb. The beauty of all is that there is no end, Kolya, to discovering beautiful, complex things. I have said enough. I tend to give speeches, so I will stop now. Do you understand me?"

"I understand you. I told you some time ago that you underestimate your intellectual strengths. I can see that, while you might still underestimate them, they are about to burst through your brain! With beautiful women, one never expects them to be brilliant and to have so much inner power."

Yvette said, "I admire many men—and women too—for their external grace, artistry, and refinement. When I discover intelligence, perception, and love underneath, I feel I have discovered gold."

They finished dinner, still on a serious note, but they were able to enjoy the ice cream.

Deciding they needed a night alone, which was mostly Yvette's decision, Kolya left soon after dinner with no physical contact. That dark and stormy expression from earlier in the day had returned, leaving his lover with a large question mark. How much did she trust this man? Did Yvette dare introduce her relationship with Abe? No! Compared to that pile of worms, Sarah was a simple complication—even if it caused a lot of pain.

Preparing for Abe's the next day was an interesting procedure. She'd told no one about Abe's advances toward her the previous week. She was unprepared, musically, with an analysis of his Trio, which she had come to love, and she was a bit embarrassed at how excited she was to spend time with Abe, despite his demands for the enjoyment of physical beauty. It was something not to be divulged to anyone, especially Kolya.

Chapter 5

On Monday evening, Kolya was in a deeply thoughtful state of mind. Having thoroughly enjoyed dinner at Yvette's, and leaving her place to walk the few steps to his own apartment, he questioned what that bittersweet sensation was which he was feeling. It was an odd sensation since they had barely touched each other since Abe's party.

He sat down in his living room and poured a glass of vintage Calvados, leaned back in his soft sofa, and enjoyed the silence and lack of chaos. The Sarah disruption had put him into a black mood for two days, which didn't often happen. To him, it meant that Yvette was more important than he'd realized. Perhaps he had taken her for granted, but that was not his usual style. She was an intriguing, gorgeous creature—such an unusual core of life and loves and passions. She was, he had to admit, a very complicated girl. Yes, she was still a girl in his eyes. Having had a baby did not turn a girl like her into a woman. Maybe she would always be refreshing, with her girlish quality sustaining that intriguing core.

He dreamed on and on about their short but intense relationship, wondering how to handle it now that Sarah had struck a bolt of lightning upon their love affair. He couldn't imagine Sarah having any influence on his affair, but Natalie was his deep secret. The symphony was his life. He had reached his goal of financially supporting himself, and that had taken so much work. He took a long sip of the brown liqueur—bittersweet was definitely reflective of his mood.

Now that I have reached one goal, and I am working hard to improve my cello playing, my chamber music projects are crucial so that I don't become another bored, boring symphony musician. Has this French delight been planted in my life to help me move ahead, see new things, and stimulate what no other person has ever been able to do? Did we jump into an intense affair too quickly? No.

She told me that her heart had to lead the way. Where do we go from here? I feel a gap in our closeness. She is passionate about her goal, and I think she can make it happen. It is an ingenious idea, but Aeschylus had the same dream in ancient history.

After another glass of his special Calvados, Kolya lumbered over to his stereo system and put on Bach's Cello Suites with Pablo Casals playing. *I will rent a car and spend all day Sunday driving Yvette to beautiful Tanglewood. If we have good weather, it would be a timely outing for us both. I think I will surprise her with this mystery on Sunday.* His black mood evaporated.

⤏ ∾ ∾ ∾ ⤎

Tuesday was Abe Day. Early March had brought the usual rain, which cleansed the streets of the winter's mud and sand. Delightful yellow and purple crocuses were barely popping through the ground, and signs of daffodils in clusters were trying to make their way toward the sun. Forsythia bushes already looked yellow, in their pre-bloom state. It was a good day to stroll slowly—under the gentle drizzle—on her favorite path up Commonwealth Avenue and through the Public Gardens. It was almost time to put away the much-worn black cashmere winter wrap and shop for a spring coat. She gave herself plenty of time to reach Arlington Street, go down Newbury Street—where there was sure to be a shop with something attractive for the new weather—and continue to Abe's.

Newbury Street was famous for its elegant boutiques, and Yvette had no trouble finding just the right one. The sophisticated saleswoman took one look at her new customer and pulled out a few spring coats. Yvette liked them all and finally chose one of a deep rose-colored gabardine that gathered at the waist and snapped up the front. There was no collar, which made it all the more stylish, pure, and simple. The fullness from the waist down to mid-calf added a dramatic flair. Deciding to wear it out of the shop, she promised to pick up her black wrap the next day. It was uplifting to head toward Beacon Hill with a new look. A teen aged boy stopped her in the Public Garden and said, "Hey lady I like your coat!" He was gone before she could respond.

Arriving on Chestnut Street for her eighth lesson with Abe, Yvette was surprised when Abe answered the door. He complimented her on her new coat. Without stepping inside, Yvette asked if they could go get an espresso on Charles Street.

40

He fumbled around to find his coat and muttered that it was a great idea.

They walked slowly down the street to find a café—Abe had a heart condition—and he asked why Kolya had been so upset.

"Abe, do you have any idea of the respect he has for you? He was quite upset that you didn't praise him and his two friends for playing your glorious Trio. He was upset that you didn't bother to go to their concert of your piece. Also, he was jealous; he had prepared me for the *womanizer* Abe."

"That's ridiculous." His light blue eyes twinkled mischievously. "Can you imagine me being such a thing?"

"*Certainement*, Abe. You are so obvious about your love for beauty. How can Beatrice bear it?"

"Beatrice and I, long ago, came to an agreement that I was allowed to behave however I chose as long as—and this is important—I never told another woman that I loved her. It sounds strange to a young thing like you—but when you are fifty years old, or more, you might understand this."

Abe's words struck her as pathetic on many levels, and it occurred to her that Abe's sole solace in the world must be his music. In that, she and Abe shared much in common.

"Does she care about the music you write? Does she focus on that?"

Abe was silent for a long moment as they walked down Charles Street.

"Oh, she has often pleaded with me to write 'something beautiful.' She sees my music as distant, interesting, and clustered ... but with no melody to carry away. Remember that she was a fine singer for many years."

"That whole thing about singing a tune as you leave a concert bothers me."

"Then we understand each other, Yvette. Oh. Here is a good place for coffee and talk." He opened the door for her.

After ordering espresso and pastries, they found a tiny table for two. The ever-perceptive Abe looked into her wide-set brown eyes and asked her to tell him everything that was on her mind.

"Oh, Abe!" She laughed. "That would take an entire day!"

"Why don't you begin now, and we can at least get started." He smirked.

"Okay. First of all, I've let you and me down in the intense study of the music you have given me."

"Nonsense. That's not true, but continue."

"I am trying to make a life that is interesting, productive, challenging, and still within my abilities. I know I am no brilliant musician, but I am a passionate one—"

"With a fabulous ear and immediate understanding of music. I am convinced the gene from Alban Berg went down the line to you. By the way, someday I have to tell you about Alban Berg. Continue please."

"I have wanted to learn so much from you about new music, but I find myself falling back on the composers I have adored for years. This weekend, there will be two performances of the Beethoven Triple, and Kolya and I will compare both versions. This is an exercise from which I get the greatest pleasure. In fact, we both do. There are times when other members of the symphony join us. We have lively discussions. This is not progressing in the direction of new music."

"Dear girl. What you are doing now is training your ear in many directions. When you are ready, and I mean really ready, you will become itching for new sounds. You already have a head start in Schoenberg's 'Verklarte Nacht.' Not many students understand that piece the way you do. It will not be long before you are ready for his other pieces that advance slowly into surprising complexities. I am convinced that you will begin to yearn for those new sounds. That is called *new* music. You must be patient and allow yourself to delve into what you love now. This will prepare you for things to come. I am old, but I have seen much. I am confident about what I see in you."

"Oh, Abe. I feel so much better already. I … really do believe in you. I trust you and respect you beyond any other musician I have ever met."

Abe took her delicate hand into his rough one.

"My professors in France don't hold a candle to what you are and what you represent. Then again, since I was studying music history and not composition, my teachers were all as stiff as sticks. Even then, I could easily see that I should have signed up for composition. It was a much more fitting ambience than what I was in. Anyway, I told you the first time we met that I always speak the truth. I even understand completely your need for sensual input in order to write these amazing pieces I have barely touched upon. I have to ask you something slightly odd … what do you think of the Beethoven Triple?"

"It is not appreciated by top musicians as being worthwhile performing. He did write the piano part for a student who commissioned the piece. It is far more technically simple than the cello and violin parts, but when a great pianist takes it on—a pianist with chamber-music sense and a colorful imagination—it can sound brilliant. But my God! What he did with the cello and violin is remarkable. And the way he weaves the orchestra into those terribly difficult parts is pure Beethoven. Pure Beethoven. Only he could have made such music. It is accessible to many, but it is never ordinary. I think this is a wonderful piece, but it is nothing like his later works. You might be enthralled when you hear it done well … if they do it well!"

"Are you a philosopher? A musician? A composer?" She tilted her head and leaned on her wrist.

He laughed. "You give me too much credit. I would love to answer that I am all of those things and more, but that would be conceited. Let's go back to my study and take a quick look at my Trio. I consider it an old piece—though I only wrote it five years ago—and I'd like you to take home and listen many times to a duet I wrote for violin and cello. It is more recent. I like it fairly well, but I'd like to know what you think of it." He murmured that he was under the spell of quite a treasure.

Yvette and Abe walked into the soft spring air and up to his study.

As Abe unlocked the door, Beatrice greeted them, asking if their walk was pleasant. She moved about the house, rearranging this and that, as if it mattered to her.

Abe and Yvette went up to his study, and he latched the door behind him.

This time, Yvette was not surprised. She asked him to play the opening of the Trio.

He replied that his fingers were badly out of shape, but he would try.

"Stop right there! What is happening?" she asked.

He told her that it was the opening motif.

"But it is so complex," Yvette said. "How can that be called a motif?"

"I didn't say it was a melodic motif. But it sets up the entire piece. Listen now."

As he played on, she began to hear some cohesive quality within. It was quite complicated, but it was just beginning to make some sense to her.

"Please play that gorgeous lyrical line that the cello has." She was sitting next to the piano. The cello line was truly magical.

Abe moved to the end of the piano bench and faced her. There was a sudden, off-putting backlash to Jacques making the first moves toward Yvette. He said, "Please let me just feel your face and your neck."

She stayed where she was and allowed him to place his hands on her hair—and then on her silken face and neck.

"I want to caress your being with a short, gorgeous piece."

As soon as he began playing, she almost shouted, "Oh Abe! That is Schumann's 'Des Abends' from his *Fantasiestuck*. It is one of the most perfect of Schumann's little pieces!"

He turned to her and held her face close to his. His kiss was more intense than any man's. She melted and felt sexually throbbing, opening her legs so he could touch her right there. Even his large hands were gentle as they massaged her genitals. She almost screamed in sexual ecstasy, but Abe covered her mouth with his. She sank back into the chair, and Abe whispered, "Quiet. Just listen now."

He played it three times.

The lesson ended with a single drop from heaven.

Yvette walked on air as she left.

Chapter 6

In spite of the perfect weather, Yvette walked faster than ever before to get back to the comfort of her apartment. She was thinking hard about all the aspects of her conversation with Abe, barely looking at her cherished buildings along the way. When she arrived and glanced at the mailbox, she was amazed to see that—instead of bills—there was a letter. Deciding to open it in her calm living room, she went up the elevator. *Hmm. Nobody ever cooks here. What is that aroma?*

She opened the door, and Kolya was wearing her apron and stirring a pot of something she'd never smelled before.

"Well, now, this is a real surprise!"

"Oh, I thought I'd surprise you with dinner cooked by me for a change. It's a typical Russian stew, borscht, but I cooked it as my mother always did. I hope you like it. How was your lesson with Abe?"

"Actually, it was different than usual, though there is never anything usual about Abe. I asked him to take me out for espresso. We had a very interesting conversation. We ended the lesson while he serenaded me with one of my favorite pieces by Schumann: Des Abends. How I adore that little gem of music."

"How was his piano playing? He used to be one of the best."

"Oh, Kolya, getting old isn't easy. His hands are quite stiff, but still there was a beauty to it which I'll never forget."

"Well, take off your new coat, which suits you perfectly, by the way. Sit down. I'll bring you a glass of wine."

"And I will read this letter from none other than Larry Stern." She flapped it to and fro in the air. "Well, I have to assume it is he since it is from the museum school."

"Good lord. He has written back! Good for him. Maybe even good for you. Tell me what he says." He pulled a chair closer to the couch and handed her a glass of crisp Pinot Grigio in her beautiful new glass. He held his glass and listened carefully.

Dear Ms. Berg,

> My colleagues and I discussed at great length the ideas in your proposal. Alas, we still could not come up with anything specific right now.
>
> However, I have an aunt who lives in Providence, Rhode Island. Isabelle Woodbridge is a widowed eighty-year-old lady who remains involved in all sorts of artistic paths. She knows everyone there, partly due to her zest for life and partly because she has been on the board of trustees of the Rhode Island School of Design. I have to admit, in spite of my love for this museum and the school we have here, the Rhode Island School of Design is probably the best design school in the country. I was telling her about you, and although her main interests are in the visual arts, she found your ideas quite seductive.
>
> A few days later, she called me and suggested that I drive you down to Providence to meet her. She has come up with an interesting idea: the summer school program is not up to the standards of the regular school-year demands, though it does attract young people who are either "trying out" the school before applying or students who simply want to study their own art at such a prestigious school. Her idea is to add a special course for you to teach music to the summer students. She was fascinated when she read that you want to start the students at their own level, find appropriate music to fit into their artistic sensibilities, and hope they catch onto something great.
>
> Could you please give me a call if you are interested? We can make an arrangement to go down for a visit with my remarkable aunt. You will find Providence quite unlike Boston. It is an interesting little city. My aunt also has an enormous home in Newport, which is about thirty minutes from the school. She would enjoy such an outing,

I am sure. In fact, she will insist that we drive and roam
through her Newport home, which is on the water.

Looking forward to your call,

Larry Stern

"Well, well, this might be just what you've been waiting for. Everything
I have heard about that school, which they all refer to here as RISD, is
quite the place. I have known Boston musicians who have gone to Newport
in the summers to play chamber music in the most amazing mansions.
Apparently, the musicians must dress in the style of the nineteenth century.
It's quite a fancy affair. Good for you, Yvette!"

"I am speechless. You are right. This could be a fabulous opportunity.
Do you mind if I take a few minutes to call my parents?"

She picked up the phone.

"Maman! Papa! Oui. Tout va bien. I just received a letter from the head
of the museum school. Non. He has nothing for me now, but his aunt has
some exciting possibilities for the summer where I would teach summer
school students just what I have in mind. This could be my entry into a real
job next fall. Yes, it is very exciting. I might need a car. Is there any chance
Papa can arrange for an old Citroen 2 CV to be delivered to Boston? It
would be the ideal car for me. I will visit this man's aunt in Rhode Island,
and she has many ideas of how to use my talents. I am very excited. Yes.
Oh, things are going very well. When can you visit? August would be very
good. But you promise to bring the Cheri painting. And I can use any other
small pieces you are willing to loan me. Is everyone well? Thank heavens.
I am trying to be economical. Yes, I am in a quartet. I am learning a lot
from Abe Lipinsky who studied with Schoenberg. He is fascinated that I
am related to Alban Berg. Well, he is a composer, yes, but he is brilliant
about all music. A critic here said that Abe's music will never be out of
fashion because it has never been *in* fashion. I have two-hour sessions with
him each Tuesday, quartet rehearsals on Wednesdays, and I go to hear the
Boston Symphony a lot. Please call me with any news. I will keep you up
to date next week. Of course I send you all my love. Goodbye.

"Now, Yvette, how are they? I am also most interested in how they met."

"Oh, they're very excited by my new life. I can't wait for you to meet
them all. My mother is the most exciting, but my two brothers are darling,

sensitive, and educated. They are not excitable like my mother. My father doesn't know what that word means, but he is a good, quiet man. He has read many books and is a deep thinker. He adores my mother, which matters so much to me. Some people find her too *alive* for their taste. Then again, they are French, and she is not! It will be such a treat for me to show them the small parts of Boston, which are my treasures."

"How did they meet?"

"I'll have to read you the letter my father sent me recently in order to do justice to their relationship. Oh, I can't find the letter. Kolya, I have been such a fool. I never asked you what you do in the summers. Does the orchestra get a real vacation?"

"Oh no. Here. Let me pour you more wine. We all gather in Lenox, Massachusetts, at a place called Tanglewood. It's our second home. The orchestra gets set up for concerts very soon after our final one here in May. It is a glorious place in the western part of the state where trees tower over everything. During the year, it rains a lot, but the summers are usually cool and lovely."

"I love this wine. But where do you live? I mean … what if I'm not in Boston and you're not in Boston? How can we keep seeing each other? I don't know how long I can go without you. What if you fall in love out there under a tree?"

He leaned back and shook his head in amusement.

"I am serious. I would miss you terribly!"

"Yvette, I feel the same. We'll arrange things. You'll have to visit me out there in my adorable apartment in an old barn. It is extremely charming … once we get rid of all the mice."

"But how do you get to rehearsals. How far is your barn from Tanglewood?"

"Every summer, I lease a car for four months, but I use it only to get from here to there and back. Here to there, I mean, the barn to Tanglewood. Would you like to drive out to see it soon? I'd be happy to rent a car and take you there."

"First, we must get a map so I can see just how far apart we'd be … if I were in Providence and you are under the trees! Also, how are you sure that you will be the one who rents it each summer?"

"The map is no problem. I have one in my apartment. When I first discovered what joining the symphony meant, I drove to Lenox in the winter to look for a small place. Yvette, it was amazing. A Russian couple who lives out there owns a farmhouse with a barn. I met the Russian in a coffee shop, recognized his accent, and we immediately engaged in a wonderful conversation. Both of us were pleased to speak our mother tongue. He asked what I was doing, and when I told him, he said he had just the place for me. Now it was no easy thing. There are many musicians looking for just what I was. But he was true to his word. We drove over to his place, and I was so enchanted. I could barely speak. He owns hundreds of acres of hilly land with a romantic little pond nestled between two low hills. I've rented that place for three summers. Vladimir and I take long walks together, and though he is not a symphony person, he loves my stories, you know, all the gossip within the orchestra. We've become very good friends. His wife, Olga, often cooks delicious Russian food for me. Sarah used to drive out to visit now and then, but she was never interested in going to concerts."

"I don't want to hear her name."

"Ah, Yvette. She did write to me recently to apologize for our abrupt ending. I only fear that she will show up unexpectedly someday. But you're not to worry. I mean that. You and I are so close after such a short time. Do you agree?"

"We haven't even kissed each other in over a week. Somehow, after seeing Sarah, I just became empty of feelings.

Sophie told me that what she and I did was called, in America, shopping therapy. It did help me feel more alive, but I certainly couldn't do my work for Abe. I was very happy to walk in and find you here. Why don't you get dinner ready, and I'll set ... oh, you already set the table. You're a darling man. Well, I'll light some candles, and we can have more of that delicious wine."

Their dinner was helpful in getting them back to where they had been before Sarah. Yvette was shocked at what a good cook Kolya was. The exotic dessert—something between a pudding and a crème brûlée topped with strawberry sauce—was unlike anything she had ever tasted.

When they had finished eating, Kolya asked her to go to her room, undress, and put on her new coat.

She raised her eyebrows and asked if he was sure that was what he wanted.

He nodded, cleared the table, and cleaned up while Yvette followed his request, taking her time. Suddenly she heard Rachmaninoff Preludes for Piano coming from the living room.

"Do you like these pieces? I'm so glad you put them on."

She stepped into the living room in her new coat, naked underneath.

Kolya looked at her intensely. "You don't know how I have missed our connection, Yvette. It got lost last week. We have to get it back."

With that, there was no more conversation. He led the way. Taking her by the shoulders, he kissed her passionately—first on her full lips and then all over her face, neck, and ears. He slowly, carefully unsnapped her coat, kissing every bit of skin that became accessible, bit by bit. Finally, the coat fell to the floor.

Yvette began to unbutton his shirt, following his lead and kissing him everywhere. She unsnapped his jeans, unzipped his fly, and pulled his pants down—and then his underwear. Feeling her way up his legs, the two of them faced each other. Silently.

Taking her hand, he led her into the bathroom, turned on the shower, and turned off the light. When the water was warm, he stepped into the bathtub and gently pulled her on top of him.

They faced each other, kissing as the warm water sprinkled over their bodies.

Yvette was completely aroused. She wanted him inside her, but he wouldn't allow that yet.

He placed her body so that her upper thighs were now at his mouth. Her little hands held onto the sides of the tub. The shower drenched them with warmth, though neither was aware of the water. Yvette's back arched in ecstasy as she begged him to get inside her.

He kept tempting her, denying her absolute sexual completion until he was ready. By then, she was crying out in physical moans and begging him to enter.

He stood up, turned off the shower, took her hand, and led her to the bed, which they saturated from their showered warmth. Finally, he entered her silken body, kissed her sweet lips, and put his hands on her buttocks.

Yvette had never before had an experience like it. She cried out in sexual exclamation many times.

Kolya shivered with pleasure as he finally completed his desires. Kissing her again between the legs, she cried out, "No more! I can't take it!" She curled up next to him and intertwined her legs with his. Both were soaking wet, sexually drained, and completely exhausted. There was nowhere to go except to sleep, wrapped into one.

On Wednesday morning, Kolya went to a rehearsal at noon. Yvette was still drunk with sex, but she managed to get in some practicing before her own quartet rehearsal.

That evening, Yvette stumbled to Kolya's quartet rehearsal. She forced herself to listen carefully. The quartet by Messiaen was special to anyone who put in time to get to know it. It was an especially remarkable quartet written in a concentration camp during WWII. A clarinet and piano filled out the four players.

As soon as the rehearsal was over, she waited for him to talk with her.

After he put his cello away, he took Yvette's hand and led the way to her apartment. They ate some leftover slices of this and that with a good baguette, talked for a long time about the quartet, had small amounts of wine, and decided to get to bed early.

She had changed the sheets, and without saying anything, they slid into her clean bed and held each other in a combination of embarrassment and thrill, not knowing what to say.

On Thursday morning, they had mostly recovered.

Yvette made espresso.

They dressed and tried to face a normal day. With each sip of espresso, she licked her forefinger and traced his lips, then licked her finger again, smiling demurely.

"When I call Larry today, will you try to join me in my trip to Providence?"

"If you make it a Sunday, I would be more than happy to be with you."

"I will make it a Sunday."

"I am able to make love to you. It is my second love-sex."

"Your second? But Sarah couldn't have been the first. So, who is the lucky lady?"

"That is a secret for another time. Back to us."

"When will I ever recover?" Yvette asked him wide-eyed, shaking her head in disbelief.

"Hopefully, never. Let me go get the map now since I have a rehearsal of the amazing Beethoven Triple concerto in half an hour."

"Oh, how is that going?"

"The pianist is becoming more alive. I think you'll hear a wonderful concert tomorrow afternoon. Do you want to sit in the balcony?"

"I'd love to sit where I heard the Schoenberg ... if that's at all possible. I really do appreciate the tickets you get for me."

51

"Every player gets a ticket for a wife or friend for every concert. I do think it's surprising that not many take advantage of that."

"So, at least I can relax, knowing that you don't have to spend money."

"Be prepared for our guest conductor. He is young and excited by having such a great orchestra under his baton. You'll hear tomorrow. I will have to take you out to dinner after it—an early dinner so I can exhaust you again, hopefully, before we go to sleep."

"No. You'll wear me out forever. We need a quiet dinner and a relaxed time afterward. Please?"

She called Larry Stern, and they decided that a week from Sunday would be a good day to go to Providence. She asked if she could bring a cellist friend, and Larry thought it would be even more fun.

"You know even eighty-year-old ladies love young men!"

Chapter 7

Friday afternoon brought the possibility of great music. Yvette wore black satin pants, a black silk blouse, and three thin gold chains of different lengths to the concert. Her seat was close to the first seat she'd had—with the red velvet railing between her and the orchestra. She noticed just how amazing a bird's-eye view of a symphony orchestra was. In France, she'd usually been in an orchestra playing her viola. Watching it from above was still a new experience.

Her eyes sweeping the orchestra, she noticed that the most dramatic section was the percussion with three huge bronze timpani in the back of the orchestra. Often the timpanist had to be a juggler to master the rapid changing of mallets within one section of a piece. Timpani are only a portion—if using more space than any other—of the percussion section. Bells, gongs, cymbals, snare drums, celestas, and glockenspiels are used in some pieces, depending on what the composers require.

Today, starting with a Sibelius symphony, there would be timpani, but in general, few percussion were used. Sibelius's style was not as dramatic as Mahler, Wagner, Bruckner, and some of the other newer composers, though his use of French horns was memorable. There were plenty of strings, brass, and woodwinds to observe with care. Sibelius's symphonies were always beautiful. This one, his fifth, was particularly beloved and well known. Yvette looked forward to it and then to the Beethoven after intermission. She watched all the musicians walking onstage slowly and chatting until they sat to focus on their business—and did they know how to focus! Kolya nodded to Yvette once he was seated, and then he joined his colleagues to warm up. Actually, though warming up might seem a minor activity, it is an essential part of getting the orchestra—and the audience—cohesive and prepared.

The young guest conductor walked up to the podium with no baton. He would clearly conduct it with his hands. The musicians looked up at him, waiting for the downbeat, which he gave in a clear, clean way. Then amazingly, he let the orchestra play the piece with surprisingly little conducting. In the Sibelius, with his long stretches of eloquence and smooth surfaces, jarred only here and there by short-lived agitation, it made sense to see and hear it conducted that way. There were no fussy beats or signals as to when different sections should enter. Every now and then, he'd move his hand to encourage them to move a bit more expressively here, a little more richly there. Yvette had never seen this done before, and the orchestra, energized by such an unusual approach, took it as a sign of his confidence in them as players who knew what to do. It was the Boston Symphony at its independent best. It was a sublime performance with a heartfelt, thrilling, and dramatic ending. The audience jumped to its feet, clapping madly and shouting, "Bravo! Fabulous!" It was the experience of a lifetime—and it wasn't even Levine or Ozawa.

Intermission was interesting. A distinguished man, sitting a few seats away, started to chat with Yvette. He offered to buy her a glass of wine, which she immediately accepted. They walked quickly to the wine bar, and he asked about her experience in music. How did she like the Sibelius? Was she excited about the Triple Concerto? Did the Boston Symphony compare to any orchestras in Paris?

Yvette found him charming, handsome, well informed, and obviously French. When the warning gong rang, they quickly went to their seats, but not before he handed her his card. Without looking, she stuffed it into her back pocket and sat down, thinking only of the upcoming music.

Now came the Beethoven Triple Concerto. Rarely performed in public, and well informed by Abe on the piece, Yvette was not distracted by her wine or the elegant man.

A baton. The Sibelius had simply played itself—and how beautifully it had played itself with little direction from the conductor's hands. No baton. This was going to be different.

It was true that Beethoven had written this piece with the finest cellist in Europe at that time, 1804, in mind. Anton Kraft had studied philosophy and law before pursuing his musical career. It made sense that Beethoven had written a particularly difficult cello part for a type of concerto that had never before been written. Yvette was all the more interested in how the cellist today, a hundred years later, would create his part. A piece of music is only as beautiful as the musician who sculpts it.

The pianist fiddled with the seat, turning this and that knob until the height felt perfect. Such an enormous, shining instrument itself was impressive. Kandinsky had been in awe of the concert grand piano years before when he heard Schoenberg's music, and as a result, he had painted a lasting painting in honor of his love of that big black piano. The violinist chose to stand, having memorized the music, so there was no need for music stands. The cellist, seated, had done the same. Now they could look carefully at each other and follow each other's musical direction.

Visually, it was rich. Both the violin and cello were of that deep, lustrous variegated brown old varnish, backed up by the giant black piano. The orchestra players were on the edge of their seats.

The conductor raised his delicate baton. The mysterious, suspenseful piece began with basses and cellists alone. As the entire orchestra entered, it worked up into an electrifying crescendo and back down to the quiet hush of the start, with just violins keeping the music going. Finally, the solo cello entered against the backdrop of the mysterious hushed violins.

Yvette's heart sank.

The violin entered a few measures later with the orchestra quietly providing the effective surrounding sounds. While the players were technically together, there was not an ounce of poetry, muscle, complete immersion, or passion to what they were doing. Yvette began to wonder why she had ever loved this piece by Beethoven. Yes, the conductor with his tiny baton was holding all of the complexity together, but it was impossible for him to force the soloists to make music out of those black dots they had memorized. Oh, how uninspired the three soloists were. There was no passion.

It was just as Yvette had predicted—a regular style of conducting. It was a technically decent performance, but it absolutely lacked the magic and the poetry she yearned for at every concert. The audience was more than elated, however. Most audiences who go to symphony concerts want to be enriched or entertained at a high level—they always loved soloists—or they had subscription tickets and went out of habit and social intercourse. The audience felt it had achieved all it wanted.

Yvette suddenly understood why audiences existed. She had never before questioned such a simple and obvious truth.

Surveying the audience and their enthusiasm, Yvette abruptly stiffened when she saw a familiar head standing to applaud. What in the world was Sarah doing here? Sarah was three rows back from the orchestra so she could watch Kolya. Yvette's insides did a somersault. How could anyone who really knew music—obviously Sarah did not—stand and applaud for such a mediocre performance? Yvette refrained from clapping.

As she stood up, her distinguished wine partner moved quickly over to her and asked her to call him sometime to discuss the concert. Yvette murmured that she would.

The magic that did occur happened when Yvette got home. She turned on the radio, and to her amazement, there was a live performance of the same Triple Concerto. It was already well into the first movement. She sat absolutely still and heard a great interpretation. What a coincidence. What a difference. It didn't sound anything like the piece she'd just heard across the street. Now she could remember why she'd loved it. Had Jacques ever mentioned the Triple in his course? Probably not since he was such a snob about introducing only the most acclaimed pieces by Beethoven. Jacques. What a mistake—a heartless intellectual. In contrast, Abe was a huge-hearted intellectual, deeper than anyone she'd ever met.

In an attempt to set aside her fury over seeing Sarah and her complete disappointment in the concert, she looked in the phone book for French restaurants. Only if the receptionist spoke French would she make a reservation. After three calls, she finally found one in Cambridge, near Harvard. Yes, seven o'clock would be fine.

She phoned Pat, and he was excited to hear her voice. He promised to pick them up in time to get to Cambridge. Throwing her pants into the laundry bag, she looked through the closet and found a shimmering yellow, sleeveless, high-collared cocktail dress, perfect for the glamorous beaded costume jewelry. She pulled her black curls into a chignon. Friday nights demanded dinner and musical discussion. How would Sarah enter the conversation? She slipped a note under Kolya's door: "Wear a jacket and tie tonight. Dinner's on me. Pat will pick us up at six forty-five."

Pat was on time. He prided himself on punctuality.

When he began to inquire about the inside of Abe's Beacon Hill house, Kolya came to life and eloquently described all the elaborate details he could remember.

"And how'd they all like yer bowl of dat stuff?"

"It was a hit, Pat. Yvette, I forgot to ask you to make another batch, much smaller, for our trip on Sunday ... our picnic in Tanglewood."

"Tanglewood? I'd love to see it. What else do we need?"

"Hey, Miss Paris, I'll bet yer handsome friend has all da rest figgered out. Am I right?"

"Pat, you're one smart cabbie. Yes, I have a delicious plan, but I need Yvette's pate."

Driving through Harvard Square was a surprise to Yvette. So many students, so many people bustling about. It had a different ambience than Boston, yet it was so close: the academic environment versus the more regular life just across the river.

"Give me a call when ya want me to pick ya up." Pat drove off.

Chez Henri's staff greeted the young couple with respect bordering on deferential regard. They were seated at a cozy table in a corner near a window. The fine white tablecloth, a tiny vase of fresh tulips, and the Sancerre in a silver bucket with ice started what could have been a perfect evening. The restaurant had a small, regular following, but the waiters saw this couple as different—more regal than their usual guests. Being treated as royalty turned dinner into an event until, after three glasses of wine, Yvette blurted out, "What was Sarah doing at the concert today?"

Kolya assured her that he had not seen Sarah, but he had been afraid she might show up anytime now that she knew he was involved with a gorgeous young woman. He tried to reassure Yvette that Sarah was in the past.

"She's not as much in the past as you'd like to think. She's after you. I can feel it."

"She can't have me. She can't get me. She is in the past, Yvette."

"She's smart and cunning."

"She is smart and cunning and heartless. Can you believe I was with such a cold fish for two years?"

"Well, you were with her for almost two years. Whatever came over you to stay with her?"

"Whatever kept you with Jacques? And, Yvette, he was married!" Yvette's face was blank, expressionless, and turning deep red.

"I can't answer that. It was such an amazing mistake. It started when I was enchanted by his knowledge of Beethoven. Before I met Abe, I was sure Jacques was brilliant. Now I can see that he knew a lot, but he doesn't even come close to Abe in intelligence." Bursting into tears, she started a stream-of-consciousness monologue about betraying her only child, getting

57

pregnant when she never wanted to be, falling in love too easily with Kolya, getting too close to Abe, and allowing music to take over her life.

She was out of control, and the restaurant asked if they needed a taxi. Pat was called.

Yvette was held up by two waiters as she staggered toward the door.

Kolya paid the bill for an unbegun, unfinished dinner. Pat arrived and looked horrified when he saw her condition. Everyone helped Yvette into the cab, and Pat knew better than to ask any questions.

The ride back to the apartments was a continuation of an incoherent babbling mixed with tears. Kolya paid Pat, who still looked aghast, and said if there was anything he could do they should just call.

On her bed, Yvette asked Kolya to tell her the story of his life. He was happy to comply.

Kolya had grown up in a small city, Gorky, not far from Moscow. A violin repair shop owner named Serge discovered Kolya's talent early on. At six years old, he went to the shop many times a week, fascinated by this man's work: cutting open the various instruments, like opening up an oyster, scraping off all the old glue, and carefully painting around the edges with the warm glue. Serge matched up all the edges before clamping them with wooden vices. Little Kolya asked all sorts of questions as he watched Serge working his spell.

Serge loaned him a cello when he was only eight years old and found a teacher for him since Kolya's parents were completely preoccupied by their teaching and political involvements. They were not aware of the talent or the musical possibilities for their only son. In fact, they had hoped he'd take an interest in studying science and go into medicine or physics.

Kolya's cello teacher decided that he should go to Paris when he was a few years older. He should live there and study with Charles Parmentier. His parents were not happy with this idea, but they agreed to consider it after his cello teacher spent hours at the Brodsky's home. He explained to them, over a long dinner prepared by Natalyia, what great possibilities lay ahead for their son. He continued informing them that money was not an issue due to the Russian government's interest in producing stellar musicians. He had confidence that this boy would be a star and that the government would subsidize his education in Paris. The Brodskys were skeptical, but they promised Kolya that they would agree to this plan if he did well in his regular studies.

Eventually, though he practiced hours every day, Kolya became fascinated by his courses in philosophy, political science, and Greek literature. He graduated as the top student.

Moving to Paris at seventeen was truly difficult. His parents had accompanied him, approved of the living quarters the conservatory provided, and helped to set him up with French lessons. He thought they even took some pride and pleasure in discovering France themselves.

"So, you see, Yvette, coming from a small Russian town, in a family where I was the only child, with parents who were detached and not emotional or loving, I had music and books to provide me with a foundation. It was not easy. You come from a much closer and loving family. They care about you in a way I've never known. In Paris, I used to think my heart would break. When I started to make a few friends, life turned a corner. I was able to discover happiness, especially when I started having girlfriends. Growing up in Russia makes one suspicious of everything. I found a more lighthearted freedom in France. I would never live in Russia again."

"But that isn't even a possibility now that you are in one of the three best orchestras in the world."

"Anything is possible, but the choices we make are what determine our happiness."

She told Kolya she needed solitude to recover from the afternoon and the Sarah incident. He crept out and let her have her quiet time alone. She was aware of how emotionally dead she was, and sleep was the best and most soothing cure.

Yvette spent the next day doing chores, listening carefully many times to Abe's Duet, and preparing her pate. As she began to do a load of laundry, she pulled her satin pants out and remembered the card in the back pocket.

Maurice Durup
French Consulate General
Boston, Massachusetts
Telephone: 617-728-1354

Oh my! He's really French. She posted the card on her refrigerator with a magnet, slipped into her pink robe, and waited on the couch for Kolya.

The door was left ajar. He walked in looking quite dashing in the evening concert uniform of black tie, crisp white shirt, and well-fitting black suit. He plunked down on the couch and stretched out his legs.

Yvette asked him how the concert had gone and handed him a glass of cold and refreshing German Riesling. "No Sarah tonight?"

Kolya shook his head. "The Sibelius went as beautifully as before. What a remarkable conductor to be so brave as to allow us to make the music! I listened to the Beethoven with your ear tonight, Yvette. I have to say that though I didn't find it *dreadful*, I agree that it was passionless playing. Now, if you want passion, our final concert is going to be in three weeks. It's Mahler's Sixth Symphony. That'll please you."

But then the Symphony's Boston season would be over. They'd all be going to Tanglewood. Oh dear. She would only know about her own summer after she'd met the woman in Providence. That was a week away. A week to worry? Not tonight. No. Tonight and tomorrow were set aside to focus only on getting stabilized.

Holding his face in her two hands, she told him that she'd made the pate for tomorrow's trip. Shifting her position on the couch, she faced him. Was he tired? Annoyed with her? Had she ruined everything by her collapse last night? Avoiding all of that, he continued without comment on the night before.

"Yvette, who was playing cello in the radio broadcast yesterday?"

"Mischa Maisky. Why?"

"I've just been wondering what cellist you admired."

"It's the first time I've heard him. Mischa Maisky with Marta Argerich and the violinist, well, I couldn't hear his name. But that cellist made my heart stop: he played with *passion!*"

"I might have known. He is an incredible musician. I have to take off this tie. Do you mind? Yvette, you really do have an ear. Maisky was just under twenty years old, and because his sister had emigrated to Israel, the government, those despicable Russian bigots, wanted to punish any Jews or even family of Jews who wanted to leave the country. This all happened before I was born, but I have seen the labor camp he was put in. Imagine that he, on his way to being one of the greatest cellists, wasn't allowed to touch a cello for two and a half years. I will tell you more about him at another time."

He grabbed her body and began to try to kiss her passionately.

She remained cold and unresponsive. "No more sex until I am better."

Chapter 8

Morning came all too soon, but it was the day for an excursion to the country!

Yvette slipped out of bed, showered, and dressed.

Kolya began to wake up and smiled as he watched her move around.

She sat next to him on the bed. "We must get going."

He groaned and said, "I've no regular clothes here."

Yvette took his key and went to his apartment to pick out some jeans, a shirt, underwear, and socks. This sort of intimacy was new to her, and she felt like a criminal looking through her man's dresser. He was very organized with all the clothes neatly folded. Seeing such a masculine creature in pink pleased her. He wore a pink shirt with a dark blue sweater. Then she went to his refrigerator, pulled out anything that had the look of a picnic on it, and brought it back to her place.

"Okay, Yvette. I am ready for the day, especially with those rolls and jam. The coffee is wonderful!"

They put together their bag of lunch supplies before he went off to pick up the rented car. They were in luck with a perfect April, sunny, cool day. When Kolya returned with a convertible VW Bug, Yvette was delighted, if still in a subdued state. To have the entire sky, the entire world, surrounding her in such an adorable car was uplifting.

They loaded their food and a blanket in the back seat, and before it was noon, they were heading toward Lenox on the Massachusetts Turnpike. Yvette loved Kolya's driving. It was very much the way he did everything physical: smooth, graceful, and confident. She kept her hand on his thigh as they drove. Having the top down made conversation impossible and was a relaxing change.

Yvette took in the outskirts of Boston and the pure, natural beauty of trees coming into bloom, tossed back and forth by a breeze. The sun reflected a shimmering effect on the leaves. It was two hours before they reached the turnoff to Lenox. Curving country roads and old homes with manicured gardens here and there were a delightful—and very American—sight. More small, curving roads were covered on either side by huge, old evergreens. Now and then, Yvette spotted bushes and smaller trees with buds desperately attempting to burst open. She smiled to herself.

Here was a tiny town. Kolya slowed down considerably and began to describe where they were and what she was seeing. Again, enormous dark green trees arched high over the road on both sides. They headed down a hill and turned left into a large gravel driveway.

"Well, Yvette, this is the famous Tanglewood. Let's get out. I'll try to show you what I can."

They were able to get inside the front gate, and Kolya showed her the tent and the old house where administrative facilities were in fervent action during the summer season. Now the covered cafeteria with long benches and tables where students and members of the symphony ate their lunches. He supposed there were many friendships—and love affairs—born in this slightly shabby open-aired cafeteria. They walked across the endless lawn and down to another area of practice sheds.

Yvette admitted she'd never seen anything like it. The enormous expanses of natural beauty combined with great musical moments must make the summers truly special.

They got back into the car and drove through the countryside for a while before turning into Vladimir and Olga's property. They parked far from the house, walked down to the pond Kolya loved so dearly, and spread out the blanket in a dry area. They unloaded the delicious bits of cheeses, the pate, plates and knives, fresh bread, pickled vegetables, a variety of multicolored olives, and diced fresh tomatoes. He had some sliced meats, and Yvette was thrilled to see sliced beef tongue. He pulled out a bottle of water and another bottle of Syrah. It was too early in the season for peaches, so apples and oranges had to suffice. When a small chocolate cake appeared, Yvette clapped her hands in delight. Yvette had thought ahead to bring a handful of napkins. They kneeled, prepared their lunch, and smiled at each other.

Eventually, Kolya grabbed her hand, pulled her to her feet, and said it was time to walk around the pond.

As they strolled, Kolya said, "I have neglected to tell you that the symphony will be in New York all next week, leaving tomorrow morning. This would mean that, sadly, I can't accompany you to Providence, much as I wanted to. I hope you won't fall in love during the week."

As they rounded the sweet and sweet-smelling pond, he also explained that when he was at Tanglewood, and if she were to be in Providence, they must stay in touch and see each other as often as possible. His life there would be extremely full. There were concerts and rehearsals every day, and she had to understand that the next chapter in their romance was going to switch gears.

"Do you mean this all might just end?" Yvette stopped and dropped Kolya's hand. Her perfectly arched eyebrows went up, and her eyes opened wide.

"It won't be the same as it has been, Yvette. The convenience of living next door is going to change everything. I'll only get a day or maybe two off each week to drive to Boston and see you. I love being here, and I'd prefer to have you visit me as often as possible, but we won't know anything about your summer until it gets worked out."

"Will Sarah come here to see you?"

"I certainly hope not. But she is a loose cannon as they say in USA." He squeezed her hand. "I just want you to know what's on my mind ... now that you've seen how I live here."

"But I haven't even seen your barn yet. I have no idea how you live here," she added with downcast eyes, feeling a touch of the other night's wild emotion creeping in. "Maybe what we've enjoyed is too much to ask for. Greedy. Is that the word? Maybe sex is our real and only strong connection, and it's wearing thin."

"We've not been *greedy*. We've been extremely lucky to have had such a pure time of those things important to us both: wine, food, music, and sex. I have never enjoyed any of these as much as with you. You must keep that in your heart."

"You sound as if you're saying goodbye to me," she barely whispered.

"No. I'm just warning you that everything'll change when I move out here. Now, let's go and eat that gorgeous food."

Yvette had no appetite, but she tried hard to put on a good front. How could she be brave when her heart was breaking? Even Jacques had never come close to her heart. She knelt and put some food on the plates.

After Kolya opened the bottle of wine, they sat down as comfortably as possible.

Yvette pulled her knee-length burgundy wool cardigan around her like a blanket.

They toasted to the future and "whatever it would hold."

Kolya remained silent to allow her to process the new information.

"This wine is lovely, isn't it, Kolya?" Yvette's spirits began to lift.

They walked up the hill to the car to see his barn, and Vladimir and Olga opened the door of the house with their arms open to welcome their darling surrogate son. Everything was in Russian until they saw Yvette's face and realized she wasn't Russian. In English, Kolya introduced them to his petite beauty. Then all four went into the barn with constant apologies in Russian to Kolya that it wasn't at all ready for him.

He laughed and said, "Of course not! I won't be here for a few weeks!"

They showed Yvette around the barn. Yvette looked carefully at Olga. Before she could show any interest in the barn, she wanted to figure out just who was this extremely attractive, well-kept woman. She was probably in her early forties, and she had good skin, alert silver eyes, and thick blonde hair that was braided and twisted into a large knot at the back of her head. Walking proudly made her seem tall in her working pants and hand-knit gray sweater with tiny Russian buttons walking, like ladybugs, down the front.

Finally, Yvette focused on the barn and the rich, old brown wood everywhere. It was enormous and still had areas where horses had been in stables and hay had been piled high. There were even pitchforks leaning here and there against the wide planks of wooden walls.

When Vladimir opened a small door into the apartment they rented to Kolya, Yvette's breath was taken away. Someone with a very good eye had made excellent use of the space, putting a wooden ceiling over the bed and bath areas, but the kitchen and living room sailed up to the rafters of the barn's ceiling.

Vladimir explained that he had always admired a Russian architect who was influenced by Frank Lloyd Wright. The conflict of cultures, in the end, produced a marvel of a space. No wonder Kolya was so fond of its simplicity with rustic elegance. A gem, the likes of which she'd never before seen. She hoped desperately that he would invite her to visit often this summer.

The four of them went back to the house for tea. Their house was quite ordinary with regular walls, painted different colors in each room, carpeted floors, and figurines from Russia. Photographs of friends hung on the walls.

Yvette said, "This tea is lovely. And I'm very impressed by the apartment in the barn."

Vladimir moved to the edge of his chair and told Yvette that when they'd bought the farm from an elderly woman who had owned it for fifty years, she requested that she be able to live in the barn in simple quarters since she was suffering from aging problems. She had hired an architect, with Vladimir's help, to tuck a living area in a small part of the barn. Vladimir liked the old lady and assured her that he and Olga would be more than happy to help her out. They understood how difficult leaving a home of fifty years must be. It would also provide them with some rental income.

As soon as the papers were signed, she started working on her project, insisting to her architect that he had to design and get it built as quickly as possible. She would live down the road with a friend until it was done. The architect and contractors worked feverishly, and her little home was ready in nine months. Everyone was amazed by the beauty of such a little place and by how quickly it had been accomplished.

The Russians had overseen this woman's well-being until she died four years ago. Vladimir met Kolya just after her death and wanted him to have it. They had loved him from the moment they met him. Now they wanted to know where Yvette was from and what she planned to do this summer.

She briefly gave a summary.

"Any friend of Kolya's is a friend of ours. We hope to see you during the Boston Symphony's season. By any chance, are you a friend of Sarah's?"

"No. I've met her, but she's been in London this year." Yvette used her best manners during the interchange. After more sweet tea, they all walked down to the pond to collect the picnic remnants.

Yvette and Olga walked behind the men, and Olga whispered, "Isn't Kolya a great lover?"

Yvette shuddered before answering, "I have no idea what you're talking about. We're just friends."

Olga seemed disappointed.

Yvette was furious and had trouble walking. She decided to say nothing to anyone. She would have to be more guarded after Olga's confession. The trip had been both elating and horrid. Putting into perspective all that had happened—all she had learned in just one day—was going to take serious reflection.

It had turned chilly so the roof had to go up for their ride home. Yvette asked Kolya to take her back to Tanglewood. She wanted to take a quick walk around the grounds before heading home. Jumping out of the car, she ran to the entrance, making it clear she wanted to walk around by herself.

Within minutes, she was back in the car. Silent. He leaned over to kiss her, and she averted her face. Hurt feelings, sad information, mixed emotions after seeing the perfect country apartment, made the drive home longer than the ride from Boston to Lenox. Yvette's mind was cluttered and uneasy, and she found it easier to say nothing.

The little VW pulled over to a rest stop. Kolya got out, opened Yvette's door, unbuckled her seat belt, and helped her to a standing position against the car. He leaned his body on hers, smoothed the curls off her face and neck, traced her perfect eyebrows with his forefinger, traced her face and every crevasse with his lips, and wrapped his arms around her. "I told you that you were my angel. You are my angel. You have fine, embroidered wings, like the best woven silk Russian lace. I am a mad Russian. I am not fine, but I love fine things. Open your hand wide. This summer will offer you that many directions and more—once you spread your lace wings and fly.

"You took the first enormous step by coming to a country you don't know. Now is your chance to follow the next step. Yvette, my beautifully sculpted porcelain creature, let's go home and make the most of our time together, apart, in our heads, in our hearts." He pulled her so close that she could barely breathe.

She melted in response to his eloquence, his embrace, and his honesty. How much could she trust his honesty now?

Yvette called her parents that evening. When her mother asked if anything was wrong, Yvette answered that she'd just had a long, very interesting day and was tired. Could she call tomorrow night instead?

Kolya walked in with some borscht. "I always keep some in the freezer. This is a good night for soup. We still have some bread from the picnic. Let's eat!"

Yvette turned off all the lights and lit more candles than she knew she owned. She had showered and wore her robe while they ate and realized, maybe for the first time, how seriously torn she was about her truly first physical love relationship. Was this love or just intense lust? The factor of trust kept surfacing in her analysis.

The symphony took off for New York to play the Sibelius First Symphony and the Beethoven under the guest conductor in Carnegie Hall and Lincoln Center. Everyone in New York and Boston was dismayed over Ozawa's illness and inability to conduct the rest of the season.

Yvette wanted to plan her week. She called her parents and had a long talk about her brothers, their love lives, and their schoolwork. She asked about her mother's painting and her father's work. What was he reading? They asked her an hour's worth of questions about her own life. When she asked about the Citroen, her father couldn't stop laughing.

"My sweet Yvette ... driving that piece of junk?"

"But, Papa, I am dying for that piece of junk. It will get me everywhere I want to go or need to go."

"What about a more sensible car in America? Can't we buy a small used car there for you?"

"*Absolutement non,* Papa. I want the most shabby, lovely 2CV you can find. Send Sebastien out to look for one that works. He has his license. He can try out different ones. I beg you!"

"Great idea," Sebastien shouted from across the room. "Hey, Yvette, I'll find a multicolored one for you." They all laughed. "Or I'll paint it for you when we get there. Are American girls cute? Can you find one for me?"

This conversation started the day on a buoyant note. Her family was extremely important to her.

Now to phone Maurice Durup whose card was still on her refrigerator.

"Hello. I'd like to make an appointment to see Monsieur Durup. Could you tell me if this is possible? My name? He won't know my name, but if you say I am the French girl he met at the symphony last week, he'll remember. Yes, I will hold on."

"Well, well. My music lover, what is your name?"

"Yvette Berg. I really don't want to bother you, but I need some advice and honestly don't know who else to ask."

"Yvette. Miss Berg. You couldn't be related to Alban Berg? No! Now that is really amazing. If you could come by tomorrow at four o'clock, I can set aside an hour. After all, we must discuss that concert."

"Oh, Monsieur Durup, I am very grateful. I will see you at four. Merci beaucoup!"

Having walked hundreds of times past the consulate en route to

Beacon Hill made it an easy arrangement. She would just be on her way home from Abe's at that time. Cancelling her time with Abe had been her plan. Feeling so emotionally drained left little room for any kind of sex.

Yvette called Sophie and invited her to dinner after their rehearsal on Wednesday. Sophie was delighted. Yvette sat down to plan a menu and then practiced. She was getting back in shape on the viola, finally, after three months of unfocused practicing. She never wanted to disappoint her three companions. Their Mozart was sounding better each week. On Wednesday, for the first time, they would perform it for their coach. Having a coach was essential, in Yvette's opinion, to making it real music.

After practicing with great concentration, she decided to listen a few times to Abe's Duet for Cello and Violin. The Second Trio of his had become very much a part of her, and this Duet was more exciting with every listen. She was hearing more of his motifs here and there, and she found the cello lyricism sweeter each time. When the violin entered, it was dynamic and extremely unusual—thrilling in fact—But she was unprepared for her session with Abe tomorrow. It would have to be cancelled. Luck was on her side.

She arrived at Abe's at two o'clock.

Beatrice answered the door, looking more nervous than usual. "Yvette, I am so sorry, but Abe isn't feeling well. He asked me to tell you to call in a few days. He's very sorry about this."

Yvette graciously said she hoped he was feeling better soon. Then, with enormous relief, wondering what to do for two hours, she went to a bookstore and bought a few books. Sitting in the Public Garden, watching the pond slowly filling up for the spring, was perfect for undisturbed reading. To her surprise, she discovered that Klee was not only a musician and painter but a writer of deep thinking and a poet as well.

When her watch said it was nearly four o'clock, she wandered over to the French Consulate, one of the smooth stone, slightly ornate buildings with a large iron gate. She announced herself to the receptionist and was ushered immediately to the office of "M. Durup."

"This is such a pleasure. I never thought I'd see you again or hear what you thought of that concert. Welcome, Miss Berg."

"It is my pleasure to be here ... though talking about that concert is not really why I came."

"Why not? You didn't like the conductor?"

"I thought his Sibelius was absolutely divine. I thought the soloists in the Beethoven Triple were horrid and passionless. And they're French. How embarrassing!"

"Miss Berg, I am really shocked. So, you truly didn't like the Beethoven?"

"Not at all. I have an ear I can always trust."

"What is your background in music?"

"I have a double degree from the Paris Conservatoire in viola and music history. I actually wanted to ask you about working here this summer. Is it legal for me to teach a course in Rhode Island?"

"Wait! Did you ever take a course on Beethoven from my friend Jacques D'Argenes?"

Yvette turned scarlet. "Yes, in fact I did. He was extremely knowledgeable about Beethoven, but he neglected to mention the Triple Concerto, which I happen to love."

"So, you did know him? How fantastic! We went to school together. I always admired him greatly. He will be coming here to visit us this summer. I will have to try to arrange that you see him." She almost fainted again.

"Oh, Monsieur Durup, I am more concerned right now about legalities and suggestions for doctors and dentists! I know it sounds terribly plebian."

"Not at all. I will write a list of doctors close by, dentists too, who can even speak French! As far as legalities, my secretary will give you all the information you need."

"And insurance? If I give you my parents' telephone number, is there any chance you can inform them as to what I need? I was like a child when I left Paris, taking care of none of this, I am ashamed to say."

"But, Miss Berg, you are a child! Of course I will phone your parents. They need to know all the requirements. If I were your father, I would insist on all that."

"You're very helpful. I am so grateful. Until I looked at your card, I'd no idea that I was missing so much important information. Thank you so very much!"

"Miss Berg, before you leave, please allow me to invite you to a lecture on Paul Klee on Thursday evening. It would be a great honor if you would attend. We have champagne at six o'clock, the lecture, and then a dinner here at eight. Can you manage that?"

"I will be here, and I thank you again very much." They shook hands, and Yvette left.

After leaving the consulate's office, she wondered why she hadn't fainted when she heard Jacques's name mentioned, much less that he would be in Boston this summer—and Monsieur Durup wanted to get them together? Horror. Well, maybe she would faint if she ever saw Jacques. Heartless beast. Just how much did he know about the daughter he helped create? If she had believed in prayer, she would have prayed that it never came to pass.

Tomorrow was the day of their quartet being coached. A great coach would insist on a perfect beginning. One coach in France had made her quartet play the opening five bars of a Beethoven Op. 18 over and over for half an hour to get each player to emphasize the opening in exactly the same way. She knew all too well that she was not a great violist, but that coach had made her play better than she knew she was capable of doing. Just in case this coach tomorrow might be as good, she wanted to practice tonight. But first, there were obligations to tend to.

Going to the grocery store, Yvette bought a large amount of foods, including some she could freeze, in order to make a great dinner for Sophie. Her order would have to be delivered with the case of wines.

Before she started cooking, she phoned Beatrice to check on Abe's health. Beatrice was even more distracted and nervous than usual, but she seemed grateful that Yvette had bothered to call. Yvette asked her to tell Abe that the Beethoven was a disaster and so far from *enchanting* that Yvette could only think of Abe's words of how great the piece could have been with great soloists. Beatrice said she would pass that on and that it would please her husband greatly.

After the delivery of her purchases, Yvette cooked like mad for almost two hours. She was pleased with every dish. The chocolate mousse would surely please Sophie. It would be a night of frank discussions with Sophie about sex. Now to practice the viola.

Chapter 9

Philippe leaned into the corner and stared at Yvette. She was being introduced all around at the consulate's wine, lecture, and dinner evening. Yvette's petite body, black curls to her shoulders, and lively, wide-set brown eyes, which were enhanced by the perfectly arched, elongated eyebrows, had captivated the young man. He made no attempt to speak with anyone. He sipped slowly from his champagne glass, feeling complete simply staring at this young animated creature. In Paris for twenty years, he had never seen the likes of Yvette before. Contemplating if he wanted to attempt an introduction, he found his position in the corner just fine for now. Two walls were holding him up.

When he walked over to have more champagne, passing close enough by her to brush against her short, pale pink dress, he saw an innocence and purity that was intoxicating. When she was engaged in a conversation, all the more animated in French, she never lost eye contact and was not distractible. At functions like this, most of the crowd was watching over the shoulder of a companion to see who was more important and to try to catch that person's eye.

Maurice Durup wandered in his direction.

"Hello, Philippe. I wasn't sure if we would see you here, but what a nice surprise. There is a young woman over there who took a course with your uncle in Paris. She is the great-granddaughter of a very famous composer, Alban Berg. She is new to Boston and obviously enjoys meeting French people. Shall I introduce you?"

"Of course, Monsieur Durup. She is certainly a beauty."

"That's what I thought when I sat near her at the symphony last week. Come over, and let's do the formalities."

Philippe, with his spiked blond hair and black leather-like outfit, followed Maurice. When there was a break in the conversation, Maurice presented Philippe to Yvette. She switched the champagne from right hand to left so she could properly shake the young man's hand.

He wondered if he'd ever shaken such a tiny adult hand.

"Philippe, Yvette studied Beethoven in a class with your uncle Jacques." Yvette turned scarlet

"You mean my mother's brother? My womanizing uncle whom my mother avoids whenever possible?"

Maurice laughed and added, "Well, I wasn't aware of those complications, but I always admired him when we were at school together. I will leave you two now. Take a look at our special painting by Klee. I have to carry out my obligations." He walked away to introduce more guests to each other.

"Yvette, are you an artist—or is this simply an elegant social occasion?"

"Ah, Philippe. I am a musician. I recently bought a book of Klee's diaries and find some of his work quite delicate and appealing. I guess what most intrigues me is his struggle between being a musician, poet, and painter. Here, read this: ----------"

Philippe read: 'At times I fancied I knew how to draw, at times I saw that I knew nothing. During the third winter, I even realized that I would probably never learn to paint. I thought of sculpture and began engraving. I have always been on good terms only with music.'

Yvette asked him what he hoped to do in the United States.

Philippe said, "I'm hoping to study painting this summer with one particular teacher, whom I admire, in Rhode Island. He will interview me next week, and it will be extremely helpful if he'll take me on for a few months."

Yvette blanched. "Rhode Island? Do you mean Rhode Island School of Design?"

"Yes."

"This is quite a coincidence. I am also going to Providence to see if I can get a job there this summer introducing, what I consider 'great music' to visual artists, yes, at Rhode Island School of Design. Do tell me about their painting program."

"All I know is that I admire this one man's work. I am completely self-taught and when I saw his work, I was ashamed at how little I know. There is so much to learn, especially from him. Perhaps you have heard of him: Paul Shapiro. He made his name painting in the Southwest."

"No, I am not familiar with most American contemporary painters …
I hate to admit. Are you familiar with the great music of Beethoven and
Mozart?"

"I did fall in love with Mozart's symphonies. I am uneducated about
any others you mention since my visual interests have been uppermost in
my mind. Why do you want to teach this kind of serious music to students
who are wrapped up entirely in their artwork?"

"As I discover more and more painters who loved music, I find that I
am discovering a new world of art. Do you think I sound naive?" Yvette
turned and asked for more champagne and a few crackers.

"I am only twenty-three and have recently been discovering how little
I know in many, many dimensions. Maybe that is what education is for."

They both turned to the waiter and helped themselves to foie gras and
more champagne.

Yvette said, "Education has become—maybe always has been—bits of
information handed out. There are so few teachers who have a large view
of the world and how things connect. Some students are smart enough
or imaginative enough to make connections on their own, but for those
who don't make these connections, life is simply less exciting and less
passionate."

Yvette felt the intensity of Philippe's eyes on her. They decided to sit
together for dinner.

"Before we start dinner, tell me why your mother is so embarrassed
by her brother. Please tell me because I had an unpleasant experience
with him."

Philippe said, "Well, he has always been unfaithful to his wife, and
when my mother discovered he was seducing all his students, she was
horrified. But that's about all I really know. I've never liked him. He
seemed like an opportunist. Let's eat."

"Of course, but first we have the lecture. I'm hoping that our speaker
is knowledgeable in a broad sense. Let's get more champagne and find a
seat." Yvette led him to a man serving champagne. They asked him to pour
it to the top—and not the proper half-filled glass.

The elegant room with sky-high ceilings supported by handsome
pillars and mirrored walls all around was filled with folding chairs. The
room was packed. Yvette and Philippe sat close to the back. On the stage
was a lectern, a musical-style stand that held the small Klee painting with
colors that were elegant and muted and very difficult to see. The lecturer

had a mustache and slicked-back, thinning hair. He looked to Yvette like all the music historians she had survived over four years in music school.

She groaned and leaned over to Philippe. "This does not look good, but we'll give it a try." As she suspected, the lecturer droned on and on about the details in the Klee painting.

Yvette sighed with every boring detail. "Philippe, you'd never know Klee was incredibly interesting from listening to this!" Abruptly, Yvette sat up as she saw an Olga look-alike.

She became obsessed and ignored the lecture entirely. Insecurity overtook every nerve in her body. She pictured Kolya in bed with Olga, with Sarah, with every woman he might have enjoyed sexually. This new torture triggered too many unanswered internal questions: Did Kolya love her? What would happen this summer when she was in Providence? Did she even think she wanted to marry him, or anyone, for that matter? Was she suited to be married? When their affair had started, Yvette had been so sure that all things should be taken only day by day. Was he happy with his cello playing—or did have aspirations which he had never divulged to her?

It was too overwhelming. She stood up, disregarding any etiquette, walked to the champagne table, sat in a chair, and silently held her glass toward the waiter as she took out a pen and a piece of paper. "Philippe, please call me tomorrow morning. We need to have coffee. Here's my telephone number: 617-728-0354. You are a lovely young man. Yvette Berg." Before stumbling to grab her spring coat, she handed the waiter a ten-dollar bill, pointed to Philippe, and asked the waiter to give him the note. Then she walked to the street, hailed a cab, and went home.

Yvette pulled out a favorite CD: Maria João Pires's version of the Schubert Impromptus. This music would be calming for the ruminating she had to do. The Impromptus were a perfect combination of intellect, poetry, and passion. Pires was a Portuguese pianist with a poetic soul and fabulous technique. Yvette had discovered her on a trip to Lisbon with her family a year earlier. What a discovery! Great musicians don't surface often. It was the appropriate music for her present mood.

In her pink robe, Yvette lit a candle, poured a glass of white wine, and tried to think logically. Her emotions had gotten the better of her, and the only remedy was to try to think logically. She and Sophie had had a good conversation the night before. Yvette had demanded to know where Sophie stood in relation to sex with men and women alike, and although Sophie was very young, she was quite sophisticated in her approach to life. Yvette discovered that Sophie's relationship to sex was similar to Abe's views on sensuality. A good orgasm in any direction was a good thing.

Yvette let Sophie understand that Yvette wanted no more physical involvement, and Sophie was alarmingly cheerful and agreeable. Their discussion then went on about music overtaking one. Was it a good thing? They agreed that no one thing should consume anybody except love. Love is the universal completion of emotion, they had decided. If we love music, its reward is enormous pleasure and satisfaction—stimulation leading to many other stimulating ideas. Maybe, however, beyond love, wisdom was the goal everyone needed in order to be able to love without that love consuming a person's being. Being consumed without the ability to see all things in perspective was not a goal we should hope for, they had agreed. These were the topics tossed back and forth over the boeuf bourguignon Yvette had prepared.

She still wondered if Kolya loved her. If he did love her, was she ready for a commitment leading to marriage? Was he? Would she ever want to be a mother, and if so, would she be a good mother? If she did marry him someday, would they be good parents? Then she focused only on the music and eventually drifted off into the world of Schubert.

The phone rang, and when Kolya asked how the past evening had gone—he asked her why it was so *monumental*—Yvette told him that she had begun to doubt every nuance of their relationship. "I can't even begin to tell you how my mind was swirling with terrible ideas, terrible images. I want you to come back so we can talk."

"My beloved, naive French angel, I will see you on Sunday night. Is that soon enough? If I remember correctly, you will be in Providence on Sunday. You must come to my place. I will have some sort of dinner ready for us. Does that reassure you at all?"

"Thank you, dear Kolya. Yes. Until Sunday night, I will be thinking of you. I kiss you back, and I am very, very grateful that you called." Yvette went to sleep on her couch.

When the phone rang again, awakening Yvette from three hours of a better sleep, it was Philippe. Yvette suggested, since the cafeteria there was decent, they meet at the Museum of Fine Arts.

He agreed it was a good idea.

As Yvette walked toward the museum, she spotted the spiked blond hair. He was sitting on a step leading up to the entry. A French-style kiss on each cheek was how they greeted each other.

She observed his questioning expression and said, "You know that life is very complicated. I simply dissolved over seeing someone I didn't want to see. How was the dinner?"

"Before I describe dinner, I have to tell you that even in well-spoken French, I couldn't understand the lecture at all. I honestly have no idea what he said. Now the dinner was excellent, remarkably so. It was the best meal I've had in ages … since I can afford so little."

"Then how did you get enough money to fly over here?"

"My parents, who are amazingly supportive, saved up for this because they knew I needed more direction. If this painter does accept me, it will have to be on scholarship. That will be difficult."

"How are you getting down to Providence to meet him?"

"The bus."

Walking downstairs to the cafeteria, they chatted about simple things. They carried their trays of mediocre food to an institutional-quality table. "And where are you staying?"

"At something called the YMCA."

Just as they began to eat, Sophie waltzed into the cafeteria.

"Sophie! What are you doing here? Please meet Philippe."

"I saw you across the street and decided to join you. I hope this is okay." She smiled broadly. "I was following the spiked hair."

"Well, you won't believe it, but Philippe is here to interview at RISD next week to work with a painter this summer. Sophie, he is staying at the YMCA. He'll get athlete's foot there! Ugh."

Sophie turned to Philippe and asked if he spoke English. "Un peu."

"Well, you must stay at my place until you go. The YMCA is horrid. I mean it. I have a couch that is very comfortable, and I can teach you a few English words."

"What is this athlete's foot?"

The girls' laughter rang throughout the cafeteria.

Yvette translated Sophie's offer into French, and Philippe was taken aback by such open generosity. He also found Sophie quite attractive as she ambled over to get a bit of food. Yvette promised him, in her absence, that she was serious about her offer.

When she came back to the table, Philippe, faltering in his English, thanked her profusely. They made all the arrangements, and Sophie said that he should collect his bag at the YMCA. She would show him where to meet her that evening, adding that there was a possibly great, and free, concert at the New England Conservatory's Jordan Hall, which Yvette must come to hear. Sophie suggested that he should come to the concert if he had no plans. It was to be a Beethoven-Brahms gala. They all agreed to meet there, and Philippe added that hearing music with two real musicians would be special indeed.

While he and Yvette didn't have a chance to have a real conversation, the plan was much more appealing than talking—and how wonderful of Sophie to pull it all together. Yvette gave her a loving look as they finished lunch.

"Do you know if there is a painting here by your RISD painter?" Yvette asked.

He told her that there was one on display on the third floor. The three of them bought tickets and went up to see it.

Songbirds spoke directly to Yvette, less so to Sophie, and delighted Philippe. It was not in the abstract style familiar to Yvette but a crossover of many different styles. Full of life and color, it depicted flying angels in soft colors. She wondered if they were angels or flying creatures. The startlingly shiny miniature black birds flying in different directions, covering all spaces in between the drifting angels, added a menacing quality to the piece. No doubt that it was a very complex and interesting work of art. They all stood before it long enough, trying to take it in.

Philippe was smiling throughout and explained, as best he could, why he liked this painter as much as he did. "You know, there is a wonderful sentence from a book I read a while ago. For me, it sums up painting: 'Painting is the silence of the mind and the music for the eye.' Do you like that?"

Yvette turned to face him, after pausing to think about it, and said, "That's perfect, except this painting doesn't look like music to me."

They drifted around the museum and looked at various works, liking some and loving one or two here and there. Yvette insisted that they find the Kandinsky section. Oh! What pleasure that gave her. They agreed to go their separate ways and meet later that night. Sophie told Philippe to follow her so she could show him Jordan Hall, just across the trolley tracks, and that he should meet her at seven. Yvette kissed the two as they left and walked slowly back home. At Symphony Hall, she stopped to look at the posters of upcoming concerts.

Before going to the concert at Jordan Hall that evening, Yvette called Abe. He was feeling much better and looked forward to seeing her on

Tuesday. After practicing the viola and looking over her material for Abe's lesson, she phoned her parents. Even though it was dawn in Paris, they were happy to hear from her. Sebastien was finding a 2 CV for her, and it would be shipped as soon as possible. Yvette jumped up and down after hearing that news. She would have her own tin can, which her father called a "piece of junk," to drive around Boston—and perhaps to Providence? Tanglewood?

Deciding to spend all of Saturday preparing for the Providence trip, she prepared for tonight's concert by listening to the Brahms Sextet. His second of two Sextets—two violins, two violas, two cellos—which opened with hushed mystery, was on the program. Yvette's degree came in handy since she recalled, from a course she'd taken on Brahms, that he'd written it in response to a failed love involvement with a woman named Agathe von Siebold. He'd used the letters in her first name—minus the T—and transformed the letters into corresponding notes for the opening theme. Having begun the piece four years before his passion for Agathe became complicated, it took him five years to complete the piece due to their breakup. Upon completion, he said, "I have emancipated myself from my last love."

Brahms doubted his own accomplishments as a composer—but never his observations of people—and he was often seen as harsh in his criticisms. The warmth in all his works, his long beautiful musical lines, and consoling harmonies portrayed who he really was. If the Sextet was played well tonight, it would be a treat.

Yvette listened to the three last Beethoven Piano Sonatas played by her favorite Beethoven pianist, Richard Goode. In these pieces, there was pure elegance, lively surprises, poetry beyond imagination, and the deepest emotion. Goode was the perfect pianist for Beethoven. Though played as three separate Sonatas, they truly were one large piece for piano. Jacques had impressed on all his students how terribly important were Opus 109, 110, 111. Yvette hoped for a decent—or perhaps wonderful—pianist. She had to admit that she had learned, in depth, about Beethoven from Jacques, though even the idea that he could show up this summer had her nerves more on edge.

A light dinner before a rich concert was in order. Slices of turkey breast, tomatoes, rice, and a radish salad seemed perfect.

Chapter 10

Philippe and Sophie waited on the front steps of the New England Conservatory's performance center. Jordan Hall filled a large corner of Huntington Avenue and Gainsborough Street, just one block down from the mighty Symphony Hall, and bordered on an area that, though not considered safe, had some lovely brick town houses. Here and there, they were interrupted by abandoned houses with the rough edges of humanity wandering too close by.

Her friends greeted Yvette, and they went inside, taking advantage of a place where the free concerts were open to the public. It allowed faculty, students, and famous musicians a chance to perform. It was one of Boston's favorite performance facilities, and the wooden pews stretching across the large, simple, and unpretentious space gave Yvette and Sophie a wide array of choices to sit for optimal hearing ability. Their expectations were high, and they filled Philippe in on what he was about to hear. Sophie was less familiar with the three sonatas than Yvette, but her knowledge of the Brahms Sextets was surprising.

Sophie was a talented violinist with a promising career and had played more chamber music than Yvette. Chamber music trains musicians to listen and play with more attention than is required by orchestral playing. Between the two girls, Philippe had a quick, in-depth lesson in music.

Beethoven was first on the program. When the pianist walked onstage, he stood before the Steinway concert grand piano and bowed to his audience. His black silk shirt and dark pants made him look avant-garde.

The girls were ready for the Beethoven threesome. They rested their elbows on their knees and focused on the music.

Philippe watched Yvette closely as she listened. She had porcelain skin, dark eyes, small hands, and a sensuous mouth. Sophie was the exact opposite of Yvette: long, messy blonde hair falling freely and covering some of the fuller features and darker skin. Everything about Sophie was rounder, softer, more spontaneous than her French friend. She was a cross between a painting by Cranach the Younger and a portrait by Manet. Sophie was physically attractive, but Yvette was more French and more classically beautiful. Seated between these two beauties at a concert was a complete delight.

The audience had been extraordinarily quiet and maintained a knowing and polite silence throughout the piano pieces. Then the audience was as ebullient as it had been silent just minutes ago.

Yvette and Sophie crossed over Philippe to hug each other in deep satisfaction and joy. Then they hugged Philippe. Sophie clung to him and kissed him on the cheek.

Yvette felt their attraction and—while thinking that she was not a jealous person—wondered if she were jealous or just pleased.

Intermission at Jordan Hall offered intimate exchanges between strangers in the audience but no wine. Philippe stood close to Sophie, and she leaned against him and asked if he was okay. He gently squeezed her arm in response.

A musician had to learn a piece to the core by rehearsing it many times. Yvette had never played either of these expanded string pieces, yet she enjoyed hearing them and knowing about them from her studies at her own conservatory. It was obvious, though, that the students at the New England Conservatory were superior musicians to her experience in France. She had become wonderfully familiar with "Verklarte Nacht" in Paris with her group there.

Philippe seemed distracted, which convinced Yvette all the more of what she had to do if she got the job at RISD. Capturing the untrained ear would be a real challenge. Her preparation for the meeting with Isabelle Woodbridge was going to take her all day: thinking, planning, and writing up a sensible proposal.

Agreeing that they had to sit down over tea at Sophie's to talk about the concert, they linked arms, Philippe between them, and walked happily down Huntington Avenue. Yvette had not been to Sophie's since the night of her first emotional collapse. Was she going to feel comfortable? Of course she would. With the company of these two interesting friends, it would be a treat to sit and speak slowly enough for Philippe to understand their analysis of the performances.

However, entering Sophie's apartment, seeing Philippe's backpack and art folio brought her to the realization that these two had set up arrangements after lunch. Then she looked at the couch where she and Sophie had reached a physical intimacy, which she had never experienced before. Jealousy? She had never before known jealousy until Kolya because Jacques had been her only lover—and he was married with children. Yvette knew what she was doing. Or did she? *Can you think you are in love and yet never feel jealous?*

"Yvette, tea or wine?" Sophie asked.

"If you have any wine, I would love a glass," Yvette replied.

"Philippe?"

He asked for some chamomile tea. In French, he asked Yvette if she loved the concert.

She answered that they all had to discuss it in English. It would help him.

"Sophie. Did you love the concert?"

"Philippe, there are so many parts to say, 'I loved' or 'I didn't love.' Where do I begin?"

Sophie was more than happy to fill him in on life in America.

Yvette was more than happy that Sophie took over this job.

Suddenly remembering where Sophie's mouth had been disoriented Yvette. She became less and less confident as Sophie's monologue continued. Yvette began to think that her own sexuality had begun with Kolya, but it was taking on different angles and proportions. He would be home on Sunday. Could she wait that long? Did she need him? Did she need Abe's unusual approach to physical attention? Disturbed by these thoughts, Yvette abruptly stood up, feeling extremely insecure, thanked Sophie for the wine, and said she must get home to prepare for her interview.

Sophie and Philippe wished her the best and asked her to phone when she found time to give a report.

Yvette walked out into the oncoming spring air, feeling sexually charged. Attempting to be logical—to suppress her physical state—was impossible. Would Sophie and Philippe have great sex that night?

Arriving at her apartment, she showered and got into her bed. Despite all her confusion in the past two hours, she slept well until a nightmare woke her up. Her daughter and she were walking across a street in Paris, and a car swerved onto the sidewalk, killing her daughter. Yvette woke up in a sweat, trembling, touching this and that to be sure it was a nightmare. It took some time for Yvette's nerves to settle.

On Saturday morning, Yvette concentrated on her discussion about music and art and how they intersected. She had to let Isabelle know exactly what she hoped could happen and also what might happen.

Larry Stern called to confirm their date at eleven o'clock.

Determined not to phone Sophie, she focused only on her presentation. She wrote down careful notes and took breaks to listen to some of her favorite music. Abe had played a role she never imagined was possible in how she listened to everything. He was the intellect of a lifetime! Was her brain possibly increasing in size with the effect of his expansive knowledge and demands?

She took herself out to dinner at Kolya's little South End restaurant. Greeted as if part of the family, Yvette felt fortunate to spend a few hours eating and drinking. They all wondered where her man was and took her under their wing when they understood that he'd been gone all week.

She felt loved and bolstered up for her visit to Providence.

Larry arrived promptly at eleven to find Yvette ready and dressed properly. A light, loose, black knee-length skirt with a plum-colored long-sleeved sweater and some gold chains with small, matching earrings had felt right for the day. Yvette loved wearing lipstick that matched her outfits.

Larry was greeted by a plum-colored, open smile. He was driving a comfortable, large car.

Yvette tucked her small box of chocolates for Isabelle into the bag with her notes.

"I only have a few CDs of your music for our trip. I hope you like the selection."

Yvette sighed with relief that conversation with him was not going to be necessary.

The drive wasn't nearly as long as Yvette expected. Within an hour, they drove up a tree-lined street and entered a pebble-crunching circular driveway.

Larry parked and said, "Here we are." He had not been talkative for an hour.

The house was formidable with its large, white-pillared front, yellow-painted clapboard exterior, and long, dark green shutters to the sides of each window.

She asked Larry if it was an American mansion.

He said that Isabelle's real mansion was in Newport, but this could be called a large New England house.

Yvette had seen similar homes in the Berkshires—and Lenox with Kolya—but nothing quite like this. They walked toward the front door, and a tall, gray-haired woman flung open the door. Her flowered dress blew around her, and she stretched out her arms outstretched in welcome. "Larry! It's been too long! I am so pleased you're here." She hugged him warmly and shook Yvette's hand. "Well, here we have a most interesting young lady from Paris. Welcome! Come inside for lunch. It's all ready."

The grand house—with high ceilings, exquisite antiques, modern paintings, and sculptures everywhere—was almost like a museum.

Yvette asked Larry if he had grown up in this house or one like it.

Isabelle said, "Larry's mother and I were very different. We adored each other, but Lucy, bless her soul, had a more traditional approach in everything she did. Larry looked at much more traditional art growing up. I used to tell Lucy to spruce things up with this or that, but she was a stubborn child and a stubborn woman. I'm just lucky I found a husband who shared my taste for great variety!"

They stopped to wash their hands—even the towels were ironed linen—and went into the dining room.

"I always think it's such a waste not to use a dining room. So, we're eating here. Even when I'm alone, I choose this." She laughed. "Yvette, do you find that ridiculous?"

"I think it's very sensible, especially when you have such a glorious dining room," Yvette answered, noticing the large, beautifully polished wooden table. Each place mat was different. None of the eight chairs matched, but the individual gems blended in their own way with the table and the fine room. Isabelle was a real character.

"Larry, you sit there. Yvette and I will be on either side of you. You must help yourself to the sandwiches and lemonade. I want to hear all your news."

Larry relaxed a bit for the first time in front of Yvette. He told Isabelle all about the museum and the struggles and joys they were having with various exhibits. He went on for a long while describing the renovation he and his male partner were doing to their home in Weston. Yvette discovered to her surprise that Larry was "gay" as they said in America. Was her one-night slip into sexual intimacy with Sophie something that made her *gay*? Isabelle wanted to hear every detail, and Larry was more than happy to fill her in. Yvette thought Larry's house sounded extremely interesting.

The food was different from any food she'd had before. She enjoyed the new flavors inside the American bread, but she didn't dare ask what it was. Isabelle had obviously squeezed the lemons for the lemonade. It was delicious with a tall sprig of mint sticking out of the top. The cut-glass pitcher oozed tiny drops of condensation. Yvette took this opportunity to scrutinize Isabelle's face. She was handsome, for sure, with gray-white straight hair poking out in all directions. For an eighty-year-old, she had unusually fine skin, an expression-filled face, and perfect posture. Her eyes were a bit like Abe's in their light blue liveliness. Isabelle had taken care in preparing this lunch.

"Now, Yvette, before we discuss your musical life, I must make some tea, which we'll have in the living room with a cake I made. I love to cook, but living alone doesn't inspire much real cooking. You two go into the living room. I'll be right there."

Trying to be polite, Yvette asked Larry about his house. He told her that someday he would have her over for dinner to show off the renovation.

They walked into another large room with paintings of all styles, colors, and sizes on the walls. Larry pointed to a Dutch still life and told her that he'd grown up with that. When his mother died, she'd left this particular one to Isabelle. He was extremely fond of it. Yvette wandered around the room, noticing every detail of furnishing, artwork, lack of knickknacks, and antique clocks on either end of the room. There were no window coverings to distract from the art. The Persian carpet was an enormous well-worn blue and gold piece. Her mother would adore this house.

Isabelle charged back into the living room, announcing that Grace would bring the tea soon. There was no couch, so Isabelle, Larry, and Yvette sat around the hand-painted coffee table.

"Now that is one of my favorite possessions," Isabelle said. "One of our RISD students made it just for me. It was a gift. Can you believe it?"

Yvette glanced at the wildly thick-stroked colors. Here and there were tiny perfectly detailed flowers: such contrast!

"He's a very talented painter who can't tolerate groups of any sort, definitely an antisocial boy who does nothing but paint. We became friends a few years ago, and I still follow his exhibits wherever they happen to be. It's a good excuse to travel." Her eyes lit up and wrinkled at the corners as she smiled. "Now, my dear, before we start dessert, I must tell you what a beautiful young woman you are—and how French you look!"

"Well, thank you, and before we start, I have this for you." Yvette handed her a small box of Godiva chocolates, beautifully wrapped, which she'd pulled out of her bag.

Isabelle gasped with delight. "Providence has no great chocolate shops, and this is a real treat." She asked Yvette about her project, explaining that music of the great masters had never been taught to her. She'd never known anyone who loved music except her young painter friend who'd given her the table. He was passionate about the turn-of-the-century composers and tried to educate her. Isabelle's music system was so outdated, and her friend had never been able to accomplish what he'd wanted for her. "Now, if you had been here, he would have had at least one friend who understood a large part of him."

Yvette said, "I know we could have become friends because finding young people who have a passion for Bach, Wagner, and Mahler is rare. It bonds the most unlikely people together."

Isabelle responded that she'd read Yvette's material, resume, and proposal very carefully, and she thought it was a fabulous idea. She had spoken to many teachers at RISD, and they all told her she would have to get a list of the summer teachers and write to them since the regular teachers weren't often the summer teachers. "Well, I did just that. I have had responses from almost all of them. They think it's a wonderful idea, but they question how you could or would carry this out. I went to the head of the summer program, Peter Long, and asked him what he thought. He told me that, as long as you would agree to a part-time position, meaning a low salary, it would be an innovative addition. You'd have to be prepared if the students weren't enthusiastic. He would like to meet you when the summer gets closer. He says he needs to know what equipment would be necessary."

"I have all that written down here." Yvette reached into her bag and handed Isabelle a thick stack of papers.

"What? You wrote this in turquoise ink by hand? I can't believe it! I absolutely adore it! I will take this to Peter this week. He'll be thrilled to see it. And I see you put down your telephone number so he can call you. Yvette, you are organized! There is one more aspect to our summers. Since you play the viola, we are always looking for musicians to play at the Newport homes. Would you consider doing that?"

"Mrs. Woodbridge, that would have to be worked out between my trips to Tanglewood. On the surface, I can say that, since my viola playing is decent, and I do love chamber music, this would be something special."

Grace walked in carrying a tray with tea and lovely, buttery mini-cakes clustered on a blue glass plate. Larry and Yvette enjoyed this treat.

Isabelle said that Yvette had to see some of the Newport homes on her next visit. "Since it is still only the middle of April, why don't you wait for a call from Peter? When you come down to talk with him about the details, I will take you on a tour."

The conversation between Larry and his aunt continued. As they prepared to head back to Boston, Isabelle warmly held Yvette's hands.

Stepping into the car, she suddenly remembered—with mixed feelings—that Kolya would be at his apartment when she returned.

Chapter 11

Looking at her calendar, Yvette noticed the weeks she and Kolya had together before he went to Tanglewood. The Mahler no. 6, final concert of the season, was coming up quickly. Maybe this was a good separation after all the outbursts and being upset over her inability to trust Kolya. Her summer was looking hopeful, and she'd asked her mother to send all the ball gowns she'd used for the large parties in Paris. She'd need them for the Newport part of her summer and the concerts she'd be playing in.

Yvette was occupied with playing her viola, studying with Abe—while trying to keep his lustiness under control—going to concerts, and meeting with other symphony musicians to discuss the concerts, accompanied by a glass or two of Martell's cognac. It was becoming more entertaining and more educational. She could feel the respect of the musicians growing. They were asking for her opinion and listening respectfully to her response. Even if there were deep disagreements, there was boundless humor among them all. It boosted her pride that the musicians were becoming her friends. She liked to call it her *group*. Once or twice, Sophie was included, but Yvette sensed their dismissal of her as just a beautiful young girl.

"Yvette, I have a really good ear, but none of your *group* is interested in my opinions."

"They are just too busy looking at your lovely face."

"Ha! They're all in love with you, Yvette."

A tiny bit of envy rose up over this. It was never spoken, but there was a silent understanding between the two friends. For weeks, Philippe had been spending all his free time with Sophie, and they had been living together as well.

Yvette and Sophie went for a long walk on Saturday afternoon. The clouds were threatening rain, but the sun was conquering the sky. The girls looked at all the shops on Newbury and Boylston Streets.

Yvette grabbed Sophie's arm and said, "Oh, Sophie! Here's a spa. It's my treat to you and me!" The peach-colored environment was calming and soothing. Sophie wanted a mud rubdown, and Yvette wanted a mint massage.

"Follow her." The woman pointed to a slender girl. She brought them to the changing rooms, and they passed through more draping cloth and into different rooms.

They undressed and used the hot tub before their massages. Soon, two young women emerged looking as unalike as two young women could.

"You look like a young pony."

"And you, Yvette, are the Thoroughbred colt."

Sophie did resemble a pony with her bronze skin, thick hair to match, and movements that were lively, unpredictable, and at times awkward. Yvette's hair fell loose and curly as she stepped gingerly, submerging her white skin and delicate limbs into the hot water. Was she embarrassed to be naked? Sophie sat next to Yvette on the rim of the pool.

Yvette playfully slid into the water only to be caught by Sophie who rubbed the delicate satin skin of her Thoroughbred from head to toe.

Yvette, not attracted at any level, couldn't reciprocate any of Sophie's moves. She eventually turned and swam to the other side of the tub to compose herself. She eyed Sophie suspiciously, trying to get a solid perspective before she was able to chat. Now that this female entanglement was clearly not what she wanted, she wondered if enjoying both Abe and Kolya was excessive. It seemed very confusing—all of it. Yvette began to wonder if she had ever been stable.

Leaving the spa, the unspoken sexual actions clouded their initially buoyant outing.

Yvette said "Look, isn't that by Philippe's painter from RISD?" The black menacing birds had caught her attention. They walked into the gallery and looked more closely. These were no *Songbirds* as labeled in the museum. As they questioned the gallery owner, they were filled in on details that Philippe had not shared.

"Does he always use black birds as a message to the viewer?" Sophie asked.

"From what he has told me, he was greatly influenced by a letter from Henry James Sr. to his sons in which he said … excuse me while I find the card. Ah! Here it is: 'Every man who has reached even his intellectual teens begins to suspect that life is no farce; that it is not genteel comedy even; that it flowers and fructifies on the contrary of the profoundest tragic depths of the essential dearth in which its subject's roots are plunged. The natural inheritance of everyone who is capable of spiritual life is an unsubdued forest where the wolf howls and the obscene bird of night chatters.'"

The girls' jaws dropped.

Sophie said, "Wow!"

They asked for a copy of the quote to show Philippe and to Kolya.

Yvette said, "Well, he is clearly a painter with a large mind."

"I'm in a state of shock," Sophie added through clenched teeth. "He certainly lives in the night with the obscene black birds." She shivered.

The girls thanked him and slowly walked out the door in somber spirits.

They saw more galleries, more opaque colors, prints, and bold shades of gray and black. Finally, a café. Espresso for Yvette. Hot chocolate for Sophie. Biscotti for both.

"This is delicious hot chocolate. Gosh, Yvette, what do you think defines a *great* artist?"

"Hmm. Well, Sophie, do you mean a great vocalist or instrumentalist or conductor?"

"It all comes down to the same thing, doesn't it? I'm asking you because I'm not satisfied with our quartet's version of the Mozart. I think we need a better musician to coach us. I haven't articulated what makes a great musician or a great painter, and I need your help. Why am I so ignorant and you are so knowledgeable? I often feel like a young child when we are together."

"Sophie, I believe that a great musician has excellent technique in whatever his or her specialty is. But way beyond that is the soul of the artist. One has to have suffered to know how to feel and interpret a given piece. You just need to listen to more and different music. We will stop at my place, and you can hear a new CD I picked up the other day. I will have to speak less, and you will understand more."

"A-ha! A mystery listen, is it? This will be fun, Yvette."

"In Paris, our quartet played the Beethoven Op. 18 no. 1, and our coach spent an entire hour on the first six notes. Imagine that, Sophie! I was so sick of those notes that I could barely face the piece later on. But the example of getting all four people to play six notes exactly together with equal emphasis on one tiny moment was a miraculous revelation for me. That was a great cellist who was a great coach. Are you familiar with singing ... I mean ... great singers and bad ones ... opera and stuff? No? All the more reason why you must listen to my latest discovery." She smiled.

Sophie seemed gloomy and not her usual self.

They were entering her apartment when Kolya opened his door. He seemed delighted to have this surprise. "So, what are you up to?"

"We've just been looking at galleries. There is so much out there, Kolya. What a fun afternoon."

"Oh, Yvette. Remember that Soulages painting you loved so much at the museum? I read a fabulous quote of how he wanted viewers of his work to feel."

"Oh! Tell us!"

"He wanted them to feel as if they had just heard a great chord struck on the piano. Isn't that just up your alley?"

Yvette clapped enthusiastically and kissed him quickly. "I am about to introduce true musicianship to Sophie via a great singer. Isn't that a fun job to do?"

"I would have to know just who you are introducing to Sophie. What if I don't approve or agree with you, Yvette?" He spread himself on the floor.

Yvette put on the CD of her new discovery: a bass/baritone singing two excerpts from Wagner's *Ring Cycle*. The warmth and perfection of his voice put Yvette into a trance. She loved it and wanted Sophie to hear such musicianship from a perfect and velvet voice. She pressed repeat, and they sat on the sofa bed. Sophie crossed her legs and curled them underneath her.

Yvette leaned back, stretched out her legs, and shut her eyes.

Kolya looked comfortable on the floor.

When Yvette turned off the CD, tears were welling up in Sophie's eyes. "Who is that?"

Kolya's excitement propelled him to his feet. "Hans Hotter. I'd know his voice anywhere. The greatest bass-baritone of all time I believe."

Yvette pulled herself into a sitting position, took Kolya's hand, and asked how he knew of Hans Hotter. She'd never heard of him until she picked up this used CD with his signature on the front page of the liner notes.

While Kolya carried on, Yvette, a bit bored by his self-satisfaction, pictured how many times she'd undressed him and turned him on and what that passion had led to. Still, in the back of her mind Olga and Sarah, in a cloudy setting, were always there.

"When I was studying cello, I sometimes played in the Opera Orchestra of Paris. I knew nothing about opera, I can tell you!" He laughed and propped his arm on a pillow. He looked so desirable, turning Yvette back into a seductress. "Once you are into the world of German opera, there are a few names considered the *real* Wagner singers. Hans Hotter is at the top with Birgit Nilsson. But, Yvette, my sweet, whatever made you choose a used CD that you knew nothing about?"

"Once a month, I make myself discover something new. When I walked into the shop, this one spoke to me. I had to buy it. What an incredible discovery!" She knit her brow in frustration. "He is *singularite ...* oh, how do you say it in English?"

"Distinctive," Kolya said.

"Well, distinctive he is. Do you agree, Sophie?"

"Yes! Yes, yes, he is distinctive, but the music plus his singing. My God ... can we listen once more?"

They sat close together on the couch and listened with their hearts while feeling the music with their brains. According to Barenboim, it was an "ideal state." A collective sigh filled the room at the end.

"Sophie, we still haven't answered you: What makes a great musician?" Yvette thought, *I wonder what Abe would have to say.* "Kolya, get ready for tonight's concert!"

"Oh. I have to go, but won't you both come to the concert tonight? We're doing a few short pieces. One is by the now-famous John Adams, and you both owe it to your musical education, as well as pleasure, to hear that, and then Brahms Fourth. The Brahms sounds extremely interesting, as does the Adams 'Short Ride in a Fast Machine.' I will want both of your opinions."

Sophie smiled.

"Here are two tickets. I'll look for you." He whirled out the door and sang his way to his apartment.

Both girls smiled and decided to change their clothes for the concert.

Sophie said, "I guess so, but my clothes are all wrong. I couldn't fit into yours. I look awful."

"Just brush your hair and put on some of my makeup. You'll look fine."

"You and your Chanel. Did you ever consider being the poster child for that company?"

Yvette suppressed a laugh. "If only! At least I'd get free samples. Let me see what you've done … Sophie the exotic. It looks great. Now it's my turn."

Yvette pulled a few strands of hair up and over and pinned them down, exposing her delicate features all the more. Yvette prepared herself with the final wool-silk, full-length pullover dress in bright blue, grabbed two colorful shawls, threw one to Sophie, and flipped one around her own body.

Yvette and Sophie had never been to Symphony Hall together. They were right over the first violins. They could barely sit still. As Yvette looked this way and that, she noticed Monsieur Durup pointing in her direction. Jumping up to see what he wanted, she tripped over Sophie and landed in the lap of an elderly couple who did not find it amusing. Yvette apologized in French, then English, then French again.

The elderly couple tightened their already pursed lips and brushed their clothes with disgust.

Monsieur Durup leaned over the furious couple and apologized to them again. "We must meet after the concert, Yvette. I have some news for you."

"Can we meet at intermission?"

"Yes. Yes, of course. I'll try to carry three glasses of wine to that door."

Sophie slid into her seat from the other end of the row.

"He is the French consulate who had the party where I met Philippe. I wonder what he wants or has to tell us. Well, let's focus on the music." Looking down, Yvette caught Kolya's eye. They smiled at each other, bringing a swell of warmth to both.

After the concert, they met outside the stage door.

"Where's Sophie?"

"The consulate, Monsieur Durup, was at the concert. At intermission, he told us that Philippe had been accepted by the painter at RISD. Sophie went flying out of the hall to find Philippe and tell him his great news. So, we are alone tonight, my beloved."

"Thank heavens. I haven't had a night alone with you for too long. Let's just go to my apartment, Yvette, and enjoy some quiet time alone." He grinned widely and wrapped his large paws around her waist.

Startled by a large flock of black birds surrounding their entry, they moved to the side door, shaking their heads at this murder of crows and trying hard to ignore it.

Yvette giggled. "Did you get your mail today?"

Since he hadn't, they both opened their little boxes.

Yvette and Kolya looked at their envelopes, at each other, and back at the envelopes. Kolya slipped his into his pocket, and Yvette put her envelopes in her purse. Finally, they got in the elevator.

In silence, they entered his apartment and hung up their coats. Kolya quietly picked out his two favorite glasses and a bottle of Calvados. The sound of the golden liquid splashing into the glass was almost shattering.

He kept flipping his two envelopes over and over until Yvette finally told him to open them. Her skin was pinched with a nervousness, which reflected in her jittery hands.

"I think we should be in our own apartments to read whatever is in these letters. Let's meet in an hour to finish the Calvados." Kolya ushered Yvette back to her place.

Opening the door, she had a feeling of dread. She sat down and opened her mother's envelope, which verified her dreadful feeling. Out fell a newspaper clipping with a photograph of a five-year-old girl playing the piano. The caption exclaimed: "Here Is the New French Child Prodigy." The article described a tragedy from a few days earlier: "Her parents died in an auto accident on the freeway just outside of Reims."

Yvette almost passed out. Her mother's note asked her if she would have any plan to take over raising the little girl. She put off the second letter until later. *One was enough!*

❦ ∾ ∾ ∾ ❦

Two apartments over, Kolya read his letter.

Dear Kolya,

It has been two years now since we have contacted each other—just as I requested—and I thank you for your patience.

I am much better and out of the hospital for a year. I would really love to meet with you soon to hear your latest news and to tell you mine. Our affair was much too good to leave hanging in midair.

I am living in the Back Bay and look forward to
hearing from you. Much love,
Natalie: 617-867-9224

Kolya was purple with embarrassment. Speechless. Sarah was a trifle, simply an inconvenience compared to Natalie.
He opened his second letter:

Dear Mr. Brodsky,

After your audition in New York, we decided that you would be a great addition to the Vienna Philharmonic. Our season begins in three months. We would be grateful for a reply from you at your earliest convenience.

Kolya felt enormously conflicted. Natalie had been the love of his life when he arrived in Boston. The Vienna Philharmonic was an absolutely top-rate, world-renowned symphony. What in the world would he do?

After an hour, Kolya went to Yvette's with Calvados in each hand. After knocking twice and no response, he went in and found Yvette on the couch.

"What was your news?"

Kolya decided only to share the invitation from Vienna.

"What will happen to us? Is this the end of my first love affair? You don't love me anymore? I am more fragile than you understand, my darling. This might be more than I can tolerate."

Kolya knew exactly what she was thinking. He had churned over this moment since he'd first shown interest in the Vienna Orchestra. Then he whispered into her ear to close her eyes and put her hands on her thighs.

Almost robotically, Yvette followed his instructions, listening to some clattering in the bathroom. He came out holding a tiny object: a little opal ring. Oh, the ups and downs of today were almost unbearable! The ring was an exquisite piece. She climbed all over his body, kissing him from head to toe and back again. He undressed, and they made love as passionately and skillfully as they had months ago. Yvette became assertive and more aggressive in her lovemaking. She demanded caresses here and there, and Kolya, enjoying this new approach, complied. Yvette completed their union, leaving Kolya in a blissful stupor.

Chapter 12

Yvette tiptoed into the living room to inspect her second letter while Kolya rested. The envelope was from France, and when she saw the return address, her stomach did a somersault. The convent was writing to her? But why? She carefully opened it, unfolded the thin paper, and read in French:

Dear Ms. Berg,

When you generously gave your baby to be in our care five years ago, we signed contracts that were strictly confidential. The couple who have been raising Chloe— that is what they named her—have kept their side of the contract. We would never intrude on your life if we didn't have extraordinary circumstances.

The fact is, Ms. Berg, Chloe's parents were killed in an automobile accident two weeks ago. It has been dreadful here at the convent with worries about Chloe who, as you will see by the attached music review, is a prodigy on the piano. The couple left a will in which they stated their wish: if anything happened to them, you would take over the care of their beloved little girl.

She is currently under our care until we hear from you. I am so terribly sorry to have to inform you of these horrid events, but here they are. We have to follow God's plan and the hope of her parents. Please telephone us at your earliest convenience—when you have had time to think this over.

First her mother's letter—and now this? She read the letter four times, trying to understand what all of it meant. Secretly, she admired her new ring.

Back in the bedroom, Kolya groaned and shifted his position.

On the sofa, wearing her pink bathrobe, Yvette wept for an hour. How could life be so cruel to her baby, the parents, and herself. What in the world should she do with this new information? How responsible could she—or should she—be? Bravely, she unfolded the newspaper article, which had a photo of Chloe at the piano.

Yvette gasped. Chloe was the spitting image of Yvette as a young child: black curls surrounding a delicate, pale, perfectly proportioned face, an elegant lace dress, and completely focused on her hands and the keyboard. The music critic couldn't rave enough about this amazing young talent. She was beyond any gifted child he'd seen before. She had the ability to be completely engrossed in the Mozart, Bartok, and various short pieces he'd never expected. To add to all of this, her technique was impeccable. And she was only five years old!

Yvette began to wail, clutching her stomach. *Oh, Lord. What am I to do?*

Kolya awakened with a start. Pulling on his pants, he moved quickly into the living room and stopped, speechless, at the sight of Yvette spinning out of control.

She screamed, "Non! We have no future! I am cursed and not up to this responsibility. I can't possibly raise a five-year-old child. Oh, God. What am I going to do? I love Kolya, and I can't leave him, but I can't desert a baby I brought into the world!" She sobbed uncontrollably.

Kolya slowly crept nearer to her—as if she were a wild tiger ready to lunge—slowly sat down next to her, and picked up the letter.

"Non! Give that to me! It is proof that we loved each other too much and now are paying a price!"

Kolya waited a long while before attempting to untangle whatever the mess was. He glanced at the newspaper article and began to see what was going on. When Yvette had cried herself into a fetal position on the couch, Kolya gently put a hand on her back and tried to soothe the terrified, miserable creature he had enjoyed beyond measure just an hour before.

When the wild sobbing turned to weeping, Kolya put her head in his lap and stroked her hair. He began to hum their favorite theme from the Rachmaninoff Second Symphony, and she quieted down into a whimpering mode.

"Do you know what my brother Sebastien said when he heard this symphony for the first time at sixteen years old?"

"No. Oh, maybe a long time ago."

"'This music reflects the agony of the soul, and it resonates in my heart.'"

"What a sensitive and precocious young man he is."

"What am I to do?" she mumbled.

"My darling, until I know what is wrong, I can hardly have an opinion or give my thoughts and advice."

"But it's too terrible to explain. Do I have to choose between you and my illegitimate baby?" She handed him the letter.

He read it in silence. Finally, in a deep, quiet voice, he said, "There is no choice to be made. If you want your little girl, that is the answer."

"But what about *us*?" she wailed.

"Well, we have no idea what will happen to us, do we? Raising your child is a sure and important commitment. Becoming the father of a child would be terribly hard for me, to be honest. Now that is my honest assessment."

"What about sex? I can't believe how we make love."

Kolya leaned his head back and couldn't stifle his roaring laughter. "Oh that? Well, no words can do justice to our great lovemaking!"

"Kolya, what do I do next?"

"You call the nuns and continue your regular life here until you know what's right. Give yourself a few days or a week or so, but let the nuns know right now what your plan is for the immediate future."

Yvette took a long, hot bath until well past midnight. She put on her bathrobe and found the phone number for the convent. Her hands trembled as she dialed her cell phone.

A woman's voice answered and asked if it was an emergency since it was only seven o'clock on a Sunday morning.

Yvette said that she had to speak to the Mother Superior immediately. Once on the line, the trembling stopped. The voice of the nun was a gentle reminder of how lovely a person she was when Yvette was waiting months to give birth. Yvette discussed her plans and asked for a little more time to know what was "God's advice." Feeling a bit guilty about using that phrase, she promised to call back in a week with an update. In the meantime, would the convent kindly and lovingly care for Chloe?

It was the first week in April, and the weather was cooperating for her walk. She dressed in a pink sweater with tiny pearls knit into it, a long string of pearls around her neck, and pink crystal earrings. After the Chanel routine, Yvette left a note under Kolya's door to tell him when she'd be back and asking if they could go out to dinner.

The spring air was energizing and refreshing to the bone. Heading down Huntington Avenue, she passed the Christian Science complex and crossed over Commonwealth Avenue at Dartmouth Street, realizing only then that she was heading for Abe.

Beatrice answered the door, looking slightly surprised, and led Yvette into Abe's study. He shouted at first that he was being disturbed, but when he looked up and saw Yvette's face, the pencil flew onto the desk. He stood up quickly, off balance at one look at Yvette. "Something is terribly wrong, Yvette. Do you want to talk here or go out for coffee?"

She slumped into her usual chair and told him everything. Everything. Abe was as intensely warm and understanding as she knew he'd be. He asked her to tell him the story of Schoenberg's "Verklarte Nacht." As she did, the parallels of that story set her mind reeling. Yes. She and Kolya were the lovers who'd met in the moonlight when the woman told the man—in the poem—that she was carrying an unwanted child and the man said to her that he'd raise the child as their own. Kolya had already said he was unable to be a father right now.

Abe impressed upon her how poignant it was that they had chosen it as their first piece to work on. Yvette had loved it. Abe, wanting privacy for his story, shut the study door and handed Yvette a box of tissues.

Yvette asked, "If you were both as disorganized as it sounds, how could you make the move, physically, to Boston?"

"I think half our belongings are still scattered over the United States." Abe laughed. Then he took on a serious tone and told Yvette that if his story had helped her to see that the bumps and twists of life are simply built into the human condition, it was probably all the advice he had to give her. Before she left, he reminded her of "Verklarte Nacht," which he found to be an uncanny parallel to her life and that of her great-grandfather's. "Schoenberg once said that the artist carries the pulse of the world within him."

Yvette's being was pulsating with wonder about Alban Berg and his youthful fathering of Albine Berg.

After thanking Abe and Beatrice, Yvette—still confused, weak, and shaking—walked back out to the bottom of Beacon Hill. Flashing memories began to explode in her head: Kolya wanting her naked, wearing only the coat; what kind of words her parents had ever used about Alban Berg, the depth of Abe and Schoenberg's intelligence; Kandinsky's passion for Schoenberg's music; her project of weaving all arts together no longer a dream: she was living it. It was a living, breathing reality. But things were so complicated right now. She thought she might die and doubled over in severe cramps, limping until she could cross the street and get to the Public Garden to sit down.

When the cramps disappeared, her brain began sorting itself into a normal mode.

Crossing over Beacon Street, through the Public Garden, and down Commonwealth Avenue, Yvette climbed up the stairs to the French consulate. Though it was Sunday, they were open for a function. Yvette went quickly to the secretary's desk. Breathless, she asked for a huge favor: "Can you make me a roundtrip plane reservation to go to Paris? I can leave any day in the next three weeks."

Chapter 13

Walking from the consulate to her apartment, Yvette stopped at a café on the sunny side of Newbury Street. Spring was blossoming in the form of colorful dresses and shirts. People were sitting and walking, smiling and laughing off the blanket of winter. Drinking coffee in the sun was a blessing.

Trying to maintain a calm deep inside to help her decide what to do had a simple effect. A word kept surfacing: Chloe, a lovely name. What would Chloe be like as a little person? Stirring her sugar into the coffee with her left hand, to watch the pretty ring sparkle in the sun, reassured her of this: Kolya and she were a team, and he seemed to want her no matter what decision she might make. But he wanted no part of fathering. She sighed. Yes, last night was exhausting. This whole new dimension was exhausting. Deciding everything was exhausting. In fact, sitting at the table in the sun was becoming difficult. Yvette put a few dollar bills under her cup and stood up.

I'm not standing. I can't breathe. Am I dying?

She slithered down onto the sidewalk.

A young man jumped and picked her up, put some sugar into a small glass of water, and told her she was having an anxiety attack. "You will feel better soon, especially if you drink this water."

Everyone at the café was jolted into action of various kinds.

"Pick her up!"

"No! Let her lie down"

The man who had rescued her told everyone to leave him to tend to her. He pulled his chair close to Yvette's to keep her stable and told her he was a doctor. "I will take care of you."

Her first glance at him was blurred by her state, but as she began to regain control, she saw how kind he seemed to be. She freely collapsed onto his sleek, elegant body.

He put a protective arm around her, helped her walk to his car, which was parked conveniently close, and placed her in the front seat. He moved deftly and assuredly, looking into her wallet to see where to take her.

The café owner started screaming and running toward them, "Her coat! Don't forget her coat!"

The doctor thanked him and placed it on Yvette's lap.

Within ten minutes, she was delivered to her apartment, leaning lightly on the doctor's arm, weeping constantly, and pressing the elevator button. After unlocking her door and hanging her coat, she meekly offered him a chair. "Who are you? You're so kind. I've no idea what happened to me." She reached for the tissue box.

"My name is Thayer Richardson, and I'm a doctor at the hospital. I was watching you as you drank your coffee. You seemed to be talking to someone ... or maybe yourself. Have you had a bad day?"

"A bad day? How about the worst possible day? I don't know what to do in the next hour, much less the next weeks. I am from Paris. I thought I knew what I was doing here, but in one day, everything has imploded. I am lost."

"Is there someone I should call? It is four o'clock, and you might be expected somewhere. Perhaps you need to talk to someone."

"I'm almost incapable of talking to you."

"Do you have any friends who could come to help? I'd rather not leave you alone right now."

"Kolya will be around eventually. Look at this ring he gave me last night."

"It's beautiful. Are you engaged then? Is that part of the problem?"

"Thayer ... Dr. Richardson, it's what happened after he gave me the ring that the problem happened. You must be a sympathetic person. Here. Read this ... maybe you'll understand."

"Hm. This is serious stuff being fired at you. Maybe you need some help from a doctor to process all that is happening and all that has happened. Would you like a referral to someone I trust completely? He's a wise old fox and would be quite the person to turn all your stuff here into some kind of opportunity. What do you say?"

Yvette laughed, surprising even herself with the harshness of her tone. "*Opportunity*? What in the world do you mean by that?"

"In Chinese, there is one word that means both *crisis* and *opportunity*. I always found that fascinating. What do you think? May I call you Yvette?"

"Oh, do call me Yvette. I'm Yvette Berg with musical connections in every pore of my body. As for the Chinese, that is really amazing because, of course, it is true that this little five-year-old prodigy could become the center of my life. I wonder if that would be fulfilling for me. Then again, who else would be better trained than I to hold the hand of this child while she seeks her musical journey? The poor little thing loses her parents in one huge bang. Horrible. I did give birth to her, and part of me thinks I owe it to her to take the best care I can. Oh, Dr. Richardson, this is all too complicated for me to be able to think clearly."

The door opened, and Kolya walked in. He seemed startled to see a man with Yvette. He walked over and firmly shook the hand of the doctor, announcing who he was. They discussed how things had ended up as they had, and Kolya thanked him, adding that he could take care from here.

The doctor scribbled down his telephone number on a scrap of paper and said to be sure to call him if necessary. With a professional, yet warm manner, he said goodbye.

Her thoughts were still tangled around her decision about Chloe. If she took over the care of her daughter, wouldn't that tie her to Jacques, whom she had come to despise? No, she would stay as far away from him as she had in the past five years. The biggest dilemma was when to go to Paris and focus her life entirely on a little girl. Would her own musical dreams vanish entirely? Maybe living with Maman could be a good thing for everyone. She leaned lazily over in bed and phoned her mother, deciding to tell her the whole story. No answer. Well, now she had more time to think it through.

After dozing off, Yvette was awakened by Kolya quietly entering the room.

"Campari and soda for the patient?" he asked.

She nodded, wondering if she was watching a movie. "Kolya, what am I going to do?"

"At the beginning of our relationship, I worried about just this sort of thing."

"I remember your warning me."

"It's entirely up to you. Having a baby is no small challenge. Perhaps taking responsibility for bringing her into the world is now the only humane choice. As for us, there are many ways two adults can work within difficult situations."

"I have been living in a dream world for years, fooling myself that I was free ... that I could do whatever I wanted. No one is free. Responsibility circles around everyone in a snakelike fashion. If you don't get trapped in one way, a different trap is just 'round the corner."

"Or, you could say that choices one makes direct one's life, and the powerful way to handle it is to let those choices be the uplifting ground on which one stands, beating the breast and daring the world to pull you down! I have done this, and I will continue to be true and grateful for all I have been given."

Yvette chuckled quietly, noting his self-satisfaction. "Well, I could never beat my breast with pride over a huge mistake I made. No, that is your method. Mine is yet to be determined."

"Was it really a mistake? Most babies are conceived consciously or subconsciously. And don't forget that it was your decision not to abort the child."

"Oh. That's a bit cruel."

"It's the truth. Even if you were living in a dream world when it happened, it was your decision."

"Well, now, I have no choice because if I stay here and pursue my career ... whatever it might be, I'll be thinking about Chloe. If I go to Paris and raise this child, I'll always be wondering what I might have become."

Kolya held her hand and said, "You can do both. You are strong and smart and talented, and you can raise this little girl and follow your own musical path as well."

The telephone rang, and it was Marie in Paris. A long conversation ensued.

Kolya waved as he left for some commitment.

Yvette poured out every detail to her mother. She knew she had a round-trip ticket to Paris soon. Her mother would pick her up at the airport, and they'd drive to the convent, spend a few days in the town, meet Chloe, and assess what should be done.

Shortly after that conversation, the French consulate called to tell Yvette that her ticket to Paris was to leave in two weeks. The adrenaline gave her the energy to get out of bed, think more clearly about her mother's advice, and leave a note for Kolya.

She went to the storage area to pull out the suitcase and prepare for her trip to Paris.

Chapter 14

Packing for spring in Paris was easy: no boots or bulky wool sweaters, but the jewelry and burgundy coat were a must. She did this without joy or excitement, but it was a job that must be done. Folding the clothes thoughtlessly was not her usual style, but in her sluggish state, it was the best Yvette could do.

Calling Abe was especially difficult until he suggested they meet at the bar near Symphony Hall. It was something to look forward to.

Kolya was not at the top of her must-do list. He had so many obligations and rehearsals, and there would be little time for them to spend together before she left. She wondered if this were an omen of what was to be: Yvette in Paris, Kolya in the United States before his voyage to Vienna in the fall. And then what?

Calls to Sophie, the conservatory, and Larry Stern kept her busy until it was time to meet Abe.

Pride in her appearance before leaving the building had always been important, but that seemed incidental with things being what they were.

When she walked into the café, Abe said, "You're in bad shape, my beautiful girl. Let's sit at that booth." The booths had smooth leather benches and worn, sticky tables.

They slid in across from each other. Suddenly, Abe leaped out of the booth and hugged a young woman who had swept in with the spring wind. "Natalie! It's been ages. How are you?"

She answered him with another hug.

Natalie, a striking beauty unlike any Yvette had met in Boston, was smiling, looking at Yvette, and waiting for Abe to introduce them.

Mario, the owner of the café, was clearly very fond of this familiar beauty. Everyone was embracing everyone else.

Abe explained that he wanted her to join them, but Yvette and he had serious business to attend to. Natalie was most understanding and kind, giving Yvette her full attention before leaving to join some symphony players at a different booth.

"Natalie is recovering from a nervous breakdown. Kolya and she were quite a couple a few years ago. Everyone assumed they'd get married, but she disappeared for a year—partly in the hospital and partly recovering. Her passion and ear for music is almost better than mine. Poor beautiful thing has had a bad time of it."

"I wonder why Kolya never talked at length about her."

"I think he was concerned that he had caused her depression, but we all know it doesn't work that way. It's mostly a genetic problem with circumstances playing a lesser role. She is a treasure, but now back to you. This is not a good situation you are in, but you must remember that you have all it takes to carry out the next step. Please don't cry. Here ... have a sip of my scotch. It works wonders in difficult times. Let's order a bit of food too. How about shrimp cocktail? Good, we'll order two."

"Abe, one of the worst interruptions this is causing is that I can't study the Mahler Sixth Symphony with you before I leave. I desperately wanted to do that and then hear it a few times by the BSO."

"Maybe all this complex stuff will be sorted out in a few weeks, and you'll be back for a while. I'd love to attend one of the Mahler performances with you. You have one of those rare astute-listening abilities." With a sweet smile, he reached across the imperfect table to hold her hand.

"What is it now? April 15? I go to Paris on April 29, and my mother and I'll get busy fixing the situation as soon as I get there ... if we can figure out where to start."

"I'll tell you what, Yvette. Tonight, I'll write a piece for this young prodigy to play. You can take it to her as an introduction ... before you tell her who you really are. I can do that and have it delivered to your apartment before you leave. You'll be taking a little piece of and by me!"

Yvette's face lit up at the thought. It would be a gentle transition from meeting this child to listening to her and admiring her expertise—if Abe's piece turned out to be playable—and then having ice cream or dinner with her mother and Chloe. She could begin to visualize something taking form.

"Now you are looking more like the beauty I know," Abe said.

105

They finished two shrimp cocktails and spaghetti and meatballs since Abe had decided that she had to have an American meal before she left.

Returning to her apartment in better spirits, though clouded by the discovery of Natalie, inspired a careful listen to her recording of the Mahler Sixth Symphony: her favorite. Maybe it could distract her from thinking about beautiful Natalie.

The opening brisk, invigorating, traditional Mahler march was a message of moving ahead: a reflection of her situation: reassuring right now, energizing, and complex while still speaking directly to Yvette's brain and heart. She found it surprising that she'd never before been aware of how many colors, sublime to coarse, was Mahler's world. He covered the spectrum of feelings and complex musical ideas in as many colors as there were on a Kandinsky palette. That artist always paired sounds with his colors. The slow movement was a refuge after the prior interesting and challenging movements. Might this be the most beautiful of all Mahler's slow movements? It was not possible to do any chores while listening through the Sixth, and Yvette was lounging in her chair when there was a knock. Expecting it to be Kolya, she slowly drew herself up and unlocked the door. What a surprise when she saw Dr. Richardson standing there, looking like an embarrassed schoolboy.

"I hope this is not a bad time, but I wanted to be sure you'd recovered enough to continue on with your complicated situation."

"Oh, Dr. Richardson! I was just consoling myself through one of my favorite pieces of music. Please come in and have a glass of wine." Yvette pulled her two beautiful antique glasses off the shelf and poured a decent Burgundy into each.

"What is this piece of music?"

Yvette sighed and shrugged. "The music is Mahler's Sixth Symphony. Have you ever heard of him? No? Well, I fell in love with him when I was twenty. He claims a symphony should embrace the entire world. His musical colors cover an entire spectrum. He's not an easy composer, but boy does he have a lot to say. The Boston Symphony is playing it for their final concert in two weeks. It will definitely be an experience! Maybe you'd like to come? I leave for Paris in two weeks—just after the Mahler concert. My mother will pick me up at the airport and help me drive to the convent where Chloe was born and then adopted, and we plan to see how that goes. I apologize for how I look. You must understand that I am not myself right now."

"Apologize? I'd imagine in your darkest hours you'd be as exquisite as now or anytime."

"I used to pride myself on looking the best possible at all times. This new development with Chloe has taken all the shine from my outside to my inner core. I wonder if I'll ever feel alive again."

"Alive and excited are elated states that few people know. For you, it is natural to be alive and excited. Of course, you'll be back to that once Chloe is in a satisfactory situation. Please call me Thayer. I'd like to know what brought you to Boston, but I must go. Could you meet me for lunch soon?"

"Where?"

"Let's see ... Café Florian on Newbury Street. On Thursday at noon?"

"Fine. I'll see you then. Thanks for stopping by." Yvette felt his hand on her arm.

Now to finish her Mahler listening and then bedtime. More exhaustion. She felt shivers from the tender touch of another human being—and a melting sensation from the feel of his perfect skin.

Reflecting on this stimulating addition to her life, Thayer Richardson, was a bit of a revelation. What a Boston-sounding name. Now night creams and bed.

The door opened noisily, and Kolya entered Yvette's bedroom. She was already sound asleep. He undressed and slipped in next to her.

Yvette awoke with an urgency that there was only a short time left in Boston, and there were so many things to take care of. In fact, there was nothing more to tend to once her suitcase was shut. She looked over at Kolya, still asleep, went to make coffee, and dressed for the day. She walked into the bedroom and placed the cup next to his side of the bed.

"What? You're already dressed? I had plans of devouring you—and now you aren't available. By the way, our rehearsal for the Messiaen Quartet went fabulously last night. That concert we give in Tanglewood is going to be something else." Kolya began to get dressed.

"I have too much on my mind to think about Messiaen. Your rehearsal isn't at the top of my list. I'm sorry. In fact, I'd be more comfortable if I had the entire day alone to take care of loose ends before I leave. Surely you must have another rehearsal for the concert tonight?"

"Of course we do, but I thought you were interested in that particular quartet."

"I am, but it's just unreal what is coming up in the next two weeks. I need to mentally get prepared. I'll see you after tonight's concert."

They kissed, and he was gone.

Shortly after Kolya left, there was a knock at the door. Beatrice was standing in the hall with a large manila envelope and a nervous smile.

"Beatrice! Please come in. How wonderful to see the personal delivery Abe promised. This is a surprise and a delight."

Beatrice wore a mauve, loose, beautifully designed dress that was reminiscent of the 1920s. She looked around the apartment and said, "Oh, my dear girl, this is not a proper place for you to live. The only work of art is that lovely piece of silk over the window. If Abe saw this, he'd insist that you move in with us!"

They chatted about the pros and cons of such conditions, proximity, and nearby symphony, and then Beatrice handed her the envelope. Eager to look at it, Yvette restrained herself to focus on hand-wringing Beatrice.

When she finally ushered Beatrice out, Yvette tore open the envelope to scan the music that had been written for Chloe. Delicate, open notes going here and there—and some chords underlying a long melody—it looked quite possible for a young person to play. She smiled at the thought and placed it carefully in the red leather briefcase with her other Abe writings and critiques. *Wait! This is by Abe's student, Cy Calogero. What happened? He called the piece* Chloe, *so he must have been filled in on her situation. There was so little time to write even a short piece for a child. Cy must be quite the musician.*

Then, as carelessly as she had packed her clothes, she now carefully placed her cosmetics and jewelry in tissue paper and then inside small satin bags.

Breathing a deep sigh, she closed the suitcase.

for Chloe

Cy Calogero

Chapter 15

Yvette thought lunch with Thayer on Newbury Street at noon sounded civilized, especially because he was such a kind and civilized person.

She didn't fuss over what to wear. She'd had too much of that sort of messiness in the past two days. Comfort was the key. Walking toward the Café Florian, Yvette was relaxed and happy to be outside. Spring really had arrived. There was so much to plan, now that she knew she had to bring Chloe back, but not today. Tomorrow she'd meet with a Realtor to find a home for herself and Chloe.

Thayer was leaning against the brick wall, looking quite handsome and reading a book when she reached the café.

"What's the book?" she asked.

"It's a story about one of your composers—Shostakovitch. Great writer, this Julian Barnes. What a time poor Shostakovich had. It has a great title too: *The Noise of Time*. Hello, Yvette. Let's go in and eat."

Thayer led her into the café with his hand lightly touching her waist.

Once seated at a fine table, Yvette examined her date's curly blond hair and carved face of true refinement. His eyes were violet blue and had a dreamy quality. He was tall and manly, but she wondered if he was fragile. No. His teeth were oddly misshapen, which only added to the personal appeal. Slim but broad shoulders topped his frame. His slender neck asked for caressing. Oh no! How could Yvette start thinking this way? She almost slapped herself to wake up to the immediate moment.

His eyes were fixed on her face. "Well, what would you like?"

They agreed to have onion soup and some bread.

It was her first experience like that with a man—no electricity zapping the air. There was a calm and serene sense of well-being. Chatting about the café and Newbury Street took most of the lunch.

Thayer, his eyes still glued to Yvette's face, said, "It seems to me you've had some pretty chaotic days recently. I wondered if you'd like to drive to a place in the country where it's peaceful and beautiful."

Yvette's face lit up and then turned dark. "As long as it's not Tanglewood."

With his reassurance, she pleasantly agreed. Everything about Thayer's movements was reassuring. There was no nervousness as he paid the bill, took Yvette's elbow as she pulled herself from the chair, and ushered her to his car.

Speaking with a soft and safe voice helped Yvette relax. Thayer described where they were going. The drive would take about an hour. Yvette sat back in the worn leather BMW seat and said, "How is it that you know this place?"

"I spent every summer here for thirty years. My mother is about to try to sell the house since my dad died. The house is enormous, and there are huge responsibilities to keep it up. You'll see soon enough, sweet Yvette."

"I am not sweet. I am a can of worms, trying to find my way out. This is the worst time in my life—except that you have come along like a knight in shining armor to help me find my path."

Now they were on one-way dirt roads, going over sand and rocks. She wondered if the old BMW would make it. Suddenly, they saw a huge pasture with a glimpse of water behind it.

Yvette suppressed anything loud and murmured about what a lovely scene it was. They turned right onto another dirt road, and in a minute, they were turning down a driveway with a very large, gray-shingled house sitting proudly in front of them.

He parked the car, helped her out, and said, "Follow me." Thayer led her around the large area, and suddenly there was the beach and water splashing on a rock wall not more than a few hundred feet away.

Yvette gasped and flew down the tiny path to the wall. She jumped onto a flat rock, sat, and stared at the water. "Where are we?"

He said, "This is one of the oldest areas for Boston individuals to take refuge from summer heat: Buzzards Bay. The enormous house is Cannon Cottage."

"You mean nobody lives here except in the summer?" she asked.

"Well, it is an exclusive and well-kept secret from the run-of-the-mill Bostonians. It used to be that you couldn't buy a house here without the approval of the old matriarch. She used to invite certain families, one at a time, for tea on her veranda. For us children, it was always thrilling to visit old Mrs. Weld. She always dressed as if it were the late 1800s, and she was extremely formal even in her expectations of children's behavior. At times, we were given a piece of candy. Now that was an important moment in our lives!"

They were sitting together on the rock, arms touching.

"Is this salt water?" Yvette asked.

"It's a bay that eventually flows into the Atlantic Ocean, but the water's pretty warm in this protected area. You are welcome to take a swim if you'd like." He grinned.

Yvette took off everything except her lacy underwear, dove into the churning waves, and started swimming like a champion.

Thayer was shocked and ran up to the house to get her a big towel.

When she emerged, like a mermaid in lace, Thayer wrapped her in the towel and hugged her from the back. After the refreshing swim, her body was pliable and relaxed.

"Thayer, how did you know this would be the perfect antidote to my past few weeks? You are a wonderful creature. Can we walk along the beach? It's empty!"

"Even in the summer, it's mostly empty. It's very private, and the people here are also private."

They strolled down the rocky, uneven beach. When the rock wall ended, they sat on the sand.

Yvette stretched out in her underwear on the towel, her tangled black ringlets dripping with salt water. "You know, in France, it's normal to be free on the beaches. I absolutely adore this feeling of freedom! thank you a million times, Thayer. What a dreadful idea to have to sell this place. It's a fabulous oasis. Can't you help to keep it up?"

He said, "There are other members of the family who'd like to see it sold. Right now, it's a tense topic when we are all together."

"Someday, Thayer, you have to give some of your past to me. You're the first real American I have met in four months. It's been nothing but music, some art, lots of passion with this and that man, all of which embarrasses me now, but I dove in headfirst. To be honest, I have learned a lot of deeply musical ideas from one other man. You are an elegant, artistic, handsome creature whose quiet presence speaks many words."

Thayer said, "When you have straightened out the Chloe situation and are back in the United States ... with Chloe I assume ... we will spend a lot of time together. I love my work as a psychiatrist, and maybe even more I love doing sculpture, but I've not had a real, loving, romantic relationship in years. I miss that. I want that. I want you to be part of that—no pressure, Yvette."

She swooned. They had started out as friends, and now there was a new possibility.

"Thayer, do you have an hour to spare tomorrow? I'd love your opinion on where I might buy a condo for Chloe and me to live in. I have an appointment with a Realtor at noon. I hate to burden you, but it would be a big help."

"I can take that as my lunch hour. Sure. I'll give you my opinion. I'll come by just before noon." He reached for Yvette's arm and slowly caressed it.

After a tour of the enormous nine-bedroom house, Yvette was taken to the barn, which was where Thayer had his sculpture studio. Yvette had to control her reaction to his amazing work. He really was a sculptor. He worked with rounded forms interlocking. She was tempted to squeal with delight, but she knew he'd be taken aback by such a response.

After they locked up the house, got in the car, and drove back to Boston, Yvette a bit itchy from the salt water on her underwear.

At noon the next day, Yvette dressed especially for Thayer and business.

After Thayer arrived, Kolya walked in and said, "Oh, it's the doctor. Well, Yvette, when you have some time later today or tomorrow, I'd like to talk to you. Good day, you two."

Thayer said, "Is that one of your headlong dives?"

"Yes … and a very complex one. He's in the symphony, and we talk shop a lot. Let's go."

The Realtor had two places to show Yvette. One was on Gainsborough Street, and it was unsatisfactory and distasteful. They went on to a newly redone condo in a brownstone on Saint Botolph Street. The workers were still putting the final touches on the inside. Yvette fell in love with it instantly. Asking Thayer's opinion was dangerous. *What if he didn't approve at all?*

Thayer smiled and encouraged Yvette to seriously consider it. He thought it was a wonderful space, and it was very large for Boston! It had three bedrooms, and was close to Symphony Hall. He particularly loved the bay window, which let in so much light.

Yvette asked the Realtor to hold it until tomorrow—after she had spoken to her father.

Thayer had to go back to work. He squeezed Yvette's hand once more and told her that it would be nice for Chloe to have room to play and play her piano. He approved without any reservations.

Back at her apartment, Kolya was waiting at her door. Yvette abruptly told him that she really had no time to talk right then.

He winced and accused her of betraying their love affair.

She said he was being selfish and greedy to need her when she had so much on her plate.

"Oh, so this doctor is on your plate now, is he?"

"Go away, Kolya. I have to buy a condo for Chloe and me. I'm in over my head with this, but I have to do it. I'll have lunch with you tomorrow."

When she told her father how much the condo cost, he was relieved. The prices in Paris were typically twice what they were in Boston. Her parents were relieved that Yvette had made a decision—as hard as they knew it was going to be. Her mother was looking forward to seeing her in less than two weeks. Papa needed the Realtor's name and number, the bank Yvette used, and other details. It looked as though it could easily accommodate Yvette and her daughter, but the furniture and other things needed to live there too!

She phoned Sophie for help, and then she phoned Larry. She thanked him for the trip to Providence and the introduction to his lovely aunt, and then she knocked him over with her latest news.

He said he was thrilled to be able to help. During the renovation of their house, a large amount of furniture and kitchen implements had crowded their garage, and they were still wondering where it should go. How wonderful that Yvette could use these castoffs. How soon could he deliver them to her new place?

Sophie returned her call with great enthusiasm that things were moving forward. She promised to help out with Chloe whenever she could, and she loved the idea that they'd be so close to the conservatory and Symphony Hall.

Dinnertime came and went. Yvette was preoccupied with all the absolutes that had to be in place before she left for Paris. She decided to keep Calogero's piece in the condo, which meant she had to find a used upright. That would be tomorrow's focus.

The conservatory's main administrative assistant was the right choice.

There would be a piano on sale since it was the end of the school year, and they always sold off a certain number of pianos. Yvette was buoyed by this information and agreed she would test out a few and choose one. The secretary wasn't sure if the timing was going to be an issue, but she promised to try her best.

Back at the apartment, there were more details to work out.

Kolya knocked on the door, and Yvette rolled her eyes. When she opened the door, his dark and stormy face greeted her. She sat him down and looked for leftovers in the fridge. Cheese and ham and bread would have to suffice.

They sat at the table, looking at their plates and then at each other.

Kolya began with the romance from three years ago with Natalie.

Yvette became impatient. "Kolya, this really is your problem. I have no advice for you. You have to work it out with her. As for Vienna, you have to see what Natalie would like to do, assuming you'd choose to be a couple. I guess I can see that we no longer have that option since she was the true love of your life. I filled in nicely in the meantime."

"Filled in? Yvette, I loved you then—and I love you now. Life has turned an unexpected corner, and between Natalie and choosing Vienna or not, I'm as dizzy as you are about your daughter. Please help me sort this out."

"No. This is your job. I have so many things to take care of. I just don't have the time to help you with your choices. You did say, a while ago, that our choices determine our happiness. Here. Eat something. That'll help. Go see Natalie. She's a beauty. I met her at Mario's Café the other night when I was with Abe."

Kolya said, "Someday, will you tell me about the Abe relationship?"

"No again. It is an ongoing brain-expanding experience, and that's all I can conjure up to explain it. He's one amazing man, the likes of which I've never met."

"Did you get seduced? Did you have sex with him?"

"Seduced? Certainly mentally. As for sex, you have been my real sexual experience." Her look softened a bit. "It has been a fabulous few months in that area."

She shooed him out to take care of his affairs and told him to remind himself of the advice he'd given her months ago.

The phone rang just in time to shut the door. Thayer asked her to dine with him, and she quickly accepted. He'd pick her up at seven o'clock.

Thayer knocked on the door, and when she opened it, he picked her up and swung her around. She laughed a happy, relaxed laugh. He commented on her lovely apricot skirt and sweater. She blushed.

They went to the Ritz and ordered lobster and champagne.

Yvette was a bit wild about such elegance and asked if he didn't have work that night.

He gave her a serious smile, shook his head, and said, "I'd *never* drink if I was about to go back to work. This is a you-and-me night." His smile softened, making his mouth look soft and kissable.

Yvette had to restrain herself again. She found his irregular teeth both a charming and a personal imperfection.

The evening progressed in a friendly manner. Sex hovered over the couple like an incandescent cloud, but it was never mentioned.

They agreed to see each other every day until she left—even if it was only for a few moments.

Chapter 16

"Hello? Yes, this is Yvette. Now? Where do I meet you? And I should ask for Mr. Harris? Fine. I'll be there in a few minutes."

The bank manager needed her to sign some papers for the purchase of the condominium. It was early in the day for business—but not too early for a banker.

Doing a quick dress-up job took a few minutes, and she emerged looking quite adult and professional. Mr. Harris was obviously pleased when he met her. They went into an office, and the door was shut. It looked like mountains of papers she had to face, but Mr. Harris assured her that these were mostly his work. She only had a few papers to sign. When he mentioned that her father was awfully generous, Yvette smiled knowingly.

The glow of last night's elegant dinner was still exuding from her being. Walking down the street, toward the Realtor, she saw Sophie. What a surprise!

"Well, Yvette, when do I get to see your new living quarters?"

"As soon as I get the keys from the agent. Come with me. You'll be happily surprised. It will be a special retreat for you during the school year. I'll get a key made for you."

Since the agent was out for a break, the girls went for coffee.

"Where have you been, Yvette? Is Kolya still on or off?"

"Kolya has many dilemmas to address. He heard from his true love, Natalie, from three years ago. She wants to see him and vice versa. Then he got an offer from the Vienna Philharmonic to join their cello section. He is really torn in many directions, and I've made it clear that I am not one of those directions. We are over, I think. I've decided to go to Paris to meet Chloe and decide when she should join me at the new condo."

"That's a pretty serious move, Yvette. How will I be able to help?"

"Only when she is here and adjusting would I ask for you to join our family. It's going to be a lot more work than I can even imagine. By the way, I've become friendly with a fabulous man who is unlike any man I've met here so far. We ate at the Ritz last night, and it was a glorious evening with no sex, Sophie! Imagine! We agreed to meet every day until I leave for Paris. Hey! How are you and Philippe doing?"

"We're pretty tight, I'd say. I almost love him. He feels the same way. But we're both so young that it's hard to predict anything. He will be in Providence this summer, and he is so happy about that: free lessons from his biggest mentor. We're getting along fine … for an unmarried couple." Sophie giggled.

When they were ready to see the new place, the Realtor reminded them how lucky they were to be getting such a beautiful condo. It was still early, and Yvette wanted to see how the light came in early in the day. They walked quickly to Saint Botolph Street, unlocked the metal gate and the front door, then climbed up a flight of stairs.

"Oh my God!" Sophie said as she walked in and danced around.

Yvette inspected the bay window. The lovely morning sunlight was streaming in.

The girls hugged each other.

The kitchen was small, but that was no problem. Three bedrooms was a huge asset for anyone trying to live in the city.

Yvette asked Sophie if she'd help on Saturday when Larry was delivering the chairs, tables, plates, glasses, flatware, and rugs. Sophie was thrilled to be asked to help. The piano was still an issue, but they decided where it should go when it arrived. There was an old-fashioned fireplace, which would easily accommodate the Duraflame logs that were easy and convenient.

Yvette locked up everything, and they walked out toward Symphony Hall, stopping at a deli to get ice cream. It reminded Yvette of her Mahler date with Abe. The concert was next weekend. Kolya most likely would not donate tickets, so she went in and bought two for Friday afternoon. Would Abe or Thayer be her partner for this fabulous experience? It would be just two days before she was off to Paris.

Back at the apartment, Peter Long called from the summer RISD program. He wanted to know what kind of equipment she would need, what kind of room might be the best, and if she had any questions.

"Peter, you are very kind to help me out. I have to go to Paris next week for family business, but when I return, I'll certainly phone you about all these questions and more. Is that all right with you?"

"Oh, yes," he said.

Yvette took a nap. About an hour later, the phone rang again. Thayer wanted to know when they'd see each other again. Yvette yawned and told him she'd be in her apartment all day and all night.

"Can I bring over some Chinese food at six?" he asked.

"That would be lovely." She would take a long bath in preparation.

Putting on her black satin pants, apricot sweater, and lots of black beads was her final preparation. Yvette was refreshed and ready.

Thayer appeared at the door just after six. He looked delectable in jeans and a starched blue shirt.

"Where ever did you find such a gorgeous belt?" Yvette asked.

"My sister sent it to me from Santa Fe. It has sterling silver buckles, which I figure is a bit over the top, but she insists on sprucing up my dress code. She's very dear to me."

"Well, it's something else, Thayer. It's beautiful in fact. Let me set up the food."

Yvette was really startled by how handsome he looked. Not bothering to warm up takeout seemed okay, so they sat down to eat with a nice glass of Chardonnay and candles.

"Yvette, I want you more than anything I have wanted in years. I'm hungry for you—not this Chinese food."

"You have me right here, right now." She smiled. "What if I want you, Thayer?"

He stood up, took her hand, led her over to the couch, and easily placed her on his lap.

She messed up his short hair and kissed his lovely hands playfully.

He placed her face between his hands, and his mouth roamed over her eyes, ears, and forehead until he reached her mouth and gave her a kiss that was more memorable than any she'd ever had. It was even more memorable than Abe's.

They kissed for a long time, tenderly, tongues intermingling, tasting each other's lips. His violet-eyed dreamy manner turned her into a sex kitten. Pulling the apricot sweater over her head, she pulled his face to her chest. He undid the lace bra and began to feel and then kiss her small, lovely breasts.

"Yvette. It is impossible that you are so perfect."

"A-ha! But you are wrong, Doctor. Just you wait and see."

"But your skin, your eyes, your eyebrows ... your neck ... the entire package ..."

She took the lead. She unbuttoned his shirt and felt his naked chest, sleek with no hair and like satin to her hands, and then she moved down to his pubic area. She could feel his engorged maleness. Unzipping his pants was tricky but worthwhile. Soft, dark blonde pubic hair surrounded a very large erection. Her hand went straight to it and massaged it gently, with her tongue flickering around where her hands left skin free.

He warned her that this would lead to ultimate intimacy if she weren't careful. He stood up and pulled off his jeans. Taking her hand again, they went to her bed. He suddenly became like an animal and moved all over her body, moaning and kissing her until they were synchronized in their breathlessness.

When they were naked, Thayer roamed with his mouth over her stomach, down to her saturated vagina, and her thighs—until she was crying out for him to finish this sweetest of all ecstasies. He thrust himself inside her, and she came in an instant as he moved back and forth.

Yvette knew to treasure this man and his skills in bed. He was simply remarkable. His hands had an exquisite gentleness. She went down to his former erection and licked him until he became excited. They performed their synchronized act again, and this time, Yvette was too excited by his presence to have another orgasm. She just wanted him to stay inside forever. She rolled onto her side, keeping him there.

He kissed her neck and shoulders and finally reached ultimate sex again.

Exhausted, they lay in bed for at least an hour before Yvette had the energy to wash herself off.

"You said you wanted me. I knew I wanted you. You are the gentlest, sweetest love-maker in the world. I want to be with you, tender Thayer."

"Well, that's easy enough to arrange. If you really mean it, I could be a renter in your condominium, but be with you every night. I would call that heaven. You must think about it and decide if it's what you really want."

Yvette asked, "Where do you live now?"

She was surprised when he answered that his mother had a large place on Beacon Hill—and he'd been staying there for more than a year. He was at work so much of the time that he didn't feel as though it was *home*. It would be such a drastic change for him to feel that he had a home and a beauty to be with every night. Now that he was thirty, he felt ready for a commitment. They'd have to work out the rental details when she was back from France. He hugged her very tightly at this new offer, new prospect, and new life.

"Well, Larry is coming at about noon. I have to decide what goes where and what I need to buy for the condo. You can always drop by if you're not busy with work. I will have Mahler Sixth ready to play as soon as things quiet down tomorrow. Sophie is also coming to help out."

"Well, I am at the lab until about two o'clock, but I'll come by as soon as I'm free."

Yvette heard a familiar sound under her door and found two tickets for the Mahler for the next Saturday night. In her nakedness, she hugged the tickets and mentally thanked Kolya for his thoughtfulness. She went back to bed with a ticket on each breast. "Thayer, we have two times to experience the Mahler world. I have tickets for Friday afternoon and Saturday night! You get to choose either or both or none at all."

Thayer and Yvette showered together and went to bed soon afterward. Yvette tidied up the sheets before getting in, and Thayer spent the night.

Chapter 17

When Larry arrived, Sophie and Yvette were waiting for him on the steps. They were in jeans, their work clothes, even though Larry had two hefty men to help carry everything up one flight and into the heavenly home.

As one piece and then another appeared inside, Sophie and Yvette were shocked at what lovely furniture they were arranging. Larry had impeccable taste in the new and the old selections. He was most impressed with Yvette's new home and promised to get her to visit his newly redone home in Lincoln. When the men had emptied the truck, Yvette gave each worker a twenty-dollar bill and overflowing thanks. She thanked Larry without the tip.

The real work was arranging everything to make the best use of the space.

Thayer arrived when they were just about done, and he had a genuine surprise in his hand: an engraved brass nameplate for her door on the outside of the building: "Y. Berg."

Yvette's body went limp over this wonderful surprise. She walked over to Thayer and hugged him hard and fast.

Sophie seemed uncomfortable around such a distinguished-looking man and left soon after the introduction.

Yvette said, "I need to buy beds for three bedrooms. Thayer, where would you go for that?"

He suggested a large outlet in South Boston, and since his car was parked in front, he suggested going right then. They held hands and walked through each room, deciding where Chloe should sleep. They needed a single trundle bed for Chloe and a queen-sized bed for Yvette and Thayer, but the third room was a puzzle. Should it be a bedroom or a piano/study room with a pull-out sofa. They headed to the bed outlet.

Yvette wanted to know what he'd been working on at the lab. He tried to explain in simple terms what experiments he and his lab partners were doing with mice to determine how much the genetic factor played a part in genes and mental illness.

Yvette listened very carefully, noting how articulate he was. "When do you see psychiatric patients?"

He said, "The weekdays are office-work days, and the people who need help somehow find me and my two office mates."

Yvette was fascinated, never having had any experience with that area of life. She was informed at length until they reached the bed outlet.

Smiling, Thayer said, "I hope that wasn't boring. There's a lot going on in the world of psychiatry, but there needs to be a lot more. Let's go inside."

Making the choices was a fairly simple affair. The trundle bed had to be comfortable in the bottom shelf. The sofa, which could turn into a bed, had to be attractive. They chose creamy velvet for that one. The queen bed had to be simple with a comfortable headrest for reading in bed. Choosing bedside tables and sheets and towels went quickly. Yvette tried to pay with her father's credit card, but Thayer got to the checkout man before she did.

"Is this going to be our first fight?" she asked, grinning broadly.

"This is only right and fair. You've outfitted your new place with lovely things, and it's time I made a contribution." He smiled and added, "Especially if I am welcome there often."

Yvette snuggled up to him and said, "You mean all the time."

They arranged a delivery date and time that was convenient for both of them and left the store.

In the car Thayer asked Yvette about where music fit into her life.

"Fit into my life? Darling, it is my life. Everything I do has something to do with this or that piece of music. Maybe this is neurotic, but there is always a piece playing in my mind. It is pleasing, but it can be annoying. That's when I put on a CD."

"But how did it all start? Not everyone falls in love with music like Beethoven and those guys."

"I can't explain it. I guess you'd have to say it's a great, generous gift. When I was just two or three, I used to draw pictures on the floor of my mother's studio. She had Bach and Beethoven and many others on her radio all the time. I absorbed it all, and when I got to be about eight, I wanted desperately to play the violin. But we all decided that the viola would be a better choice. There's no arguing over such a decision!" Yvette laughed and rubbed Thayer's neck and ears. "The viola turned out to be my instrument. When my father was taken to Boston for two years, we all went. Maman signed me up for lessons at the conservatory. I was fairly talented for a young girl. We lived on Commonwealth Avenue for those two years, and learning English took over a lot of my musical interest. I played in the conservatory orchestra and discovered a lot of orchestral stuff. Some of it was lovely, and some was just work to get through, but all of it seeped into my soul, body, and brain. Interestingly enough, both of my brothers had no interest at any level. I was committed from the age of eight."

Thayer asked her why Gustav Mahler was so important to her.

"Come to my apartment. I didn't bring my sound system to the condo. I will play just two movements from his Sixth Symphony, and I think you'll understand."

Settled in her apartment, Yvette took out her favorite version of Mahler's Sixth. "Mariss Jansons conducted this with the right dynamics, tempi, moving and retreating to make it feel just right." Yvette sat next to Thayer, holding his left hand, and started the CD. A heavy, forward-moving, strong, and weighty march began the piece. Then violins entered, singing beautifully lyrical phrases.

"Fate enters often from Mahler's own thoughts and predictions in this particular symphony. The drastic changes in major and minor keys produce intensity and a certain terror. Mahler once stated that 'an artist has the power to intuit, even to experience, events before they occur and that he cannot escape the pain of such foreknowledge.'"

Yvette shortened the first movement and went directly to the slow movement, which put Thayer in a trance. It was a balm after the complex first movement's harsh rhythmic overlaps. He obviously was enjoying the slow movement.

"Well, Yvette, this composer must reflect a lot of how you feel and think. Now that is extremely complicated. How do you live inside a body with music like that coursing through your blood? Are you sure I'm not just a boring doctor after hearing just a bit of Mahler?"

"It takes years of close listening to get to love such complex stuff. I'm three years into this, and I am just at the tip of really understanding him. But remember what I have to fall back on—Beethoven, Schubert, Brahms—all the old masters who mostly simply give immense pleasure to the ear and the soul. They're not as challenging like our Gustav here."

Thayer shook his head. "Let's get something for dinner. I need to change the tune in my head." He picked Yvette up and held her close. "Tomorrow is Sunday. I usually spend the day at the barn doing sculpture. I invite you to come down to the water and the house with me … if you don't have a lot to take care of."

"Oh, Thayer, what an invitation. Would you allow me to watch you work?"

"Only in silence. I focus ferociously when I am working. I'd like to spend the night at my mother's tonight and pick you up at ten. We need an hour alone in your place before I leave." He squeezed her thigh up high and stared at her.

After such a busy day they were both tired.

She dropped her clothing and headed toward the shower.

Thayer smiled, picked up all her clothes, and joined her in the shower.

Excitement dominated over fatigue, and they soon went straight to bed.

Thayer rubbed her little feet, pedicured in red, and then moved slowly to her vagina. He buried his entire face and breathed in her aroma. Next up to the belly, which asked for stroking with his penis. Easily done. Now to suck her breasts as she moved back and forth, asking for *real* sex.

He laughed. "What is this if not real sex?"

In silence, she took his erection and pushed it inside her. Now there were groans and gurgles and hot breathing from Thayer. He placed her on top, stopped all movements, and look carefully at her.

She closed her eyes, smiled, and rubbed his silken chest.

When they came together, Yvette began to cry. "Oh. Can we do it again? You are too lovely, Thayer."

He left her sleeping while he went home to clean up, prepare clothes for tomorrow, and get some much-needed sleep.

The beds would arrive on Tuesday, and they could be together indefinitely. Life was good.

Chapter 18

Life hadn't always been so good, so kind, and so loving to Thayer. There was a deep reason he chose to become a psychiatrist: he'd suffered childhood depression for ten years. He was so ill that he frequently couldn't go to school—or even get out of bed. He was able to do one thing: work with his hands. He made airplane models, Lego cities, and metal sculptures.

At eight years old, he'd joined an adult jewelry class. Within minutes, he had used the torch for welding small pieces of jewelry together. Those were the only things that could hold his attention. His parents were usually beside themselves because the doctors believed there was no such thing as childhood depression or ADHD. The doctors thought his mother was at fault for being overly anxious about her child.

Thayer was finally able to do schoolwork brilliantly at age eleven, but he knew all too well what the black hole of meaningless and futility and agitation meant. The deep understanding of those horrors—of that abyss—stayed with him through medical school and convinced him that he would have to become a person who could help children, adults, and senior citizens to back away from the black hole. Psychiatry seemed the path he'd need to follow.

His mother marveled at her normally serious and introverted son now whistling at home.

Monday was a workday for Thayer, and his day began at eight. He called Yvette to start her day with some affection over the phone. She was beaming at his call and told him she'd cook a light dinner for them. The lovers were both relieved to know they'd see each other. Thayer faced his day full of distraught, confused, or unhappy patients—each one of whom felt even slightly better after a session with him. They felt understood.

Yvette phoned Dr. Cohen for advice on introducing herself to her daughter. He'd just had a cancellation at three o'clock. She said she'd be there. Her list consisted of the piano, the French nanny, and a series of small chores before she left on Sunday.

She headed straight to the grocery to get dinner off her list. Her worries were decreased since Thayer had awakened her early enough to get a lot more done than if she'd stayed lazily in bed. Three o'clock was the deadline.

"I wonder if you started your sale on pianos?" she asked.

The administrator replied, "Oh, my. We are starting it tomorrow. If you'd like to try one out right now, I can give you a key."

"Thank you so much." Yvette trotted down to the basement practice rooms and looked over four of the pianos that would be for sale. One in particular took her fancy—it was a one-year-old upright Kawai, which had a more mellow sound than the other three. That was the one she wanted to buy.

The woman at the desk said, "I can't promise you anything, but if you come by at nine o'clock, you'll be the first in line for that piano. Good luck," she said with a smile.

Walking past Symphony Hall reminded her that Saturday night was Mahler and Thayer night. Friday afternoon would be Yvette and Mahler time. It would be another opportunity for comparisons in performance. Luckily, Seiji was better enough to conduct this weekend.

As she was turning the corner, she bumped into Kolya.

Yvette felt such conflicting emotions. He was cordial but not overly friendly. She handed him the ring and explained that it was meaningless now and their romance would be stored in her memory. It was a relief. She'd called Sophie to rearrange the rehearsal, and Kolya had answered the phone. More conflict was in the air.

"Yvette, the Mahler will take your heart and mind to another planet. It is going very well in rehearsal. Ozawa must be feeling a lot better. I know you won't be disappointed. Feel free to join us at the café after Friday's performance!"

"I think I will back out of Sophie's and my quartet rehearsal. It will be too tense to see her after her night with Kolya," Yvette said silently to herself.

That left Wednesday open for Thayer and her to awaken in the Saint Botolph Street condo. The beds would be delivered on Tuesday. Things were lining up, and Dr. Cohen could see her and give her advice for meeting Chloe.

Entering his office on Beacon Street was a warm and soothing experience. Dark wood paneling and watercolor paintings everywhere sent ethereal messages.

The secretary's welcome jolted Yvette back to reality.

"Oh! I was so taken by the artwork that I forgot to introduce myself. How do you do? My name is Yvette Berg."

"Yes. I see, and you lucked out with a cancellation today. The doctor will see you momentarily. Please have a seat over there."

Yvette sank into the oversized, ancient brown leather chair, giving her time to gaze around. The watercolors were not recently painted and had a sweetness and quaintness to them.

"Miss Berg?" Dr. Cohen was short and round and cheerful as could be.

Yvette jumped up and shook his warm, plump hand.

"Please come into my office."

She noticed even more lovely watercolors covering the walls in a haphazard style. "So, you like art, do you?"

"Oh, Dr. Cohen, my life is music first—and then art and love second."

"That's a pretty full life you have, Miss Berg. Thayer claims that you are a living, breathing example of how a young person should be. Now that's something, coming from the wisest young psychiatrist I know. Have a seat and let's see what I can do for you."

Yvette began to tell her story, weeping often as she explained how, why, and what had happened to her in the past five years. When she got to the Chloe part, the weeping became full-fledged crying. "What am I going to do? How do I introduce myself to my own child?"

Dr. Cohen handed her a box of tissues and continued to be as cheerful as he was during their first handshake. He calmed her down quickly with his mere presence. "Miss Berg, you have done more things, activities, and interactions than most people do in a lifetime. You need to be gentle with yourself in this traumatic meeting with Chloe. You must follow your heart when it comes to the actual event. Chloe's only five and is probably in shock right now. Tenderness, sympathy, and understanding come across quickly to a bright child. I have faith that you will know what to do only when you are faced with seeing Chloe. You might even begin the introduction by asking her to play a piano piece for you. As for what to tell her, I believe that will come to you when you have shaken her hand or lightly hugged her. She will let you know how much she can handle ... as far as real information goes."

Dr. Cohen talked at length about Yvette's plan for Paris, the condominium, and the possibility of leaving Chloe in Paris for more readjustment before bringing her to an English-speaking country.

At the end of an hour, Yvette felt more confident and more alive than before. Dr. Cohen had been extremely helpful.

The day was coming to a close. Yvette walked slowly back to her apartment, thinking over Dr. Cohen's advice. Dinner was also on her mind, but it took a very distant second place.

Chapter 19

She called Sophie about their rehearsal on Wednesday, and Kolya answered Sophie's phone again. "Well, you don't waste any time. What happened to Natalie?"

He said, "Oh, she had to go to her parents' house before we move in together. Sophie and I went dancing last night. We had a great time!"

"Hmm. Is Sophie there?"

They rearranged the Wednesday rehearsal, and Sophie sounded a bit embarrassed.

She called Abe to cancel their Tuesday time together. They had an interesting talk about the Mahler Sixth, and Abe said he was unable to accompany her. Secretly, Yvette was relieved. She'd rather go with Thayer for one performance and alone the second time.

She drifted off to sleep.

Yvette awakened with another nightmare and had to jump out of bed to regain reality. The tears flowed uncontrollably. "Chloe, I almost forgot about you!" Yvette was perspiring profusely, afraid of the dark, and didn't know how to find Chloe.

When the lights were on and things were back in place, Yvette realized it was an anxiety attack. A quick, cooling shower helped restore her to her senses. Climbing back into bed, Yvette knew she was doing too many things. She had too much responsibility. Dozing off, she dreamed of the beach and water at Buzzards Bay.

Kolya knocked on her door at nine thirty and awakened Yvette just in time for her to be ready for Thayer's imminent arrival. She sleepily asked him what he wanted.

"I've decided to live with Natalie, and I wanted you to know that."

"Kolya, that is wonderful to have made a decision and chosen a long-lost love. Congratulations. I have to go and get dressed. Have a great time today, knowing one decision is off your mind."

Thayer arrived in jeans and a work shirt. Yvette had a bathing suit, a large towel, loose pants, and an oversized shirt. They had a quick hug and then down to the car.

In the back seat, there was a large piece of granite.

"So, it's carving granite today?"

He looked at her and smiled.

The traffic wasn't bad, but it wasn't summer yet. Beginning in late June, the traffic to the "oasis" could be most annoying. Things were going their way today.

Thayer pulled out a Thermos of strong dark coffee, and Yvette pulled yesterday's French bread out of her bag.

They drove in silence for a long time. Yvette's stomach still hadn't cleared up from her attack. Should she tell Thayer? She leaned over and hugged her knees.

"A nervous stomach is part of the anxious package," he said. "It's most uncomfortable, but if you put the seat back, you might get some relief."

It worked!

Yvette decided to open up to him about her nightmare and anxiety attack.

He calmly reminded her that such things happen to highly strung, artistic souls. "Do you think you are high-strung?"

A deep chuckle emerged from her small chest. "Oh yes. I guess I've always been high-strung, but that's partly why I connect so purely with this and that music."

"That's all true enough, my perfect package, including the anxiety part." He put his hand up high on her thigh.

They drove into the dirt roads and then down to Cannon Cottage. Yvette felt more and more elated to be near open water.

Thayer parked the car and carried the granite to the barn.

Yvette flew to the water and stared at it for a long time before putting on her suit and plunging in. The tide was lower, and she was disappointed to have to walk out to the deeper part. It was still thrilling to float and swim hard and fast until she was breathless. The beach gave her a long time to think about how to manage a five-year-old.

Meeting Chloe was the initial obstacle, and that was only in a week! Leaving her towel behind, she looked up at the spotty clouds and out at the far-reaching water. She took a long walk down the beach and discovered a few small cottages. The beach turned a corner, and she sat down to contemplate the introduction to Chloe. There had always been the slim possibility that they might meet—but never under these circumstances.

Kicking seaweed and choosing pretty rocks were her activities on the way back to Cannon Cottage. "Thayer, is there water on in the house? I need a quick, even cold, shower after my happy swim."

"Just outside the kitchen door. Yes, I think the water is on."

Washing her hair and getting out the salt was a relief. Dressed now, she wandered up to the barn where there was intermittent noise from the compressor. Yvette quietly entered the sculpting area and saw that the granite work had just begun. She started to inspect the old stalls, the hayloft above the stalls, and the old ice-box. What history was embedded here!

When she stepped down into a lower level of the barn she had to cover her mouth. Sitting in disrepair was an old yellow Citroen Deux Chevaux. Yvette sat in the dusty car and shifted the gears. The roof was the old authentic pull-back style canvas. She didn't know whether to laugh or cry. It was a more important discovery than she could have hoped for. Listening for the compressor to pause, she ran up the barn stairs and burst into tears. "Thayer, you have the one treasure I have dreamed about! I want it so badly ... my brothers were arranging to ship one to me!" She wiped the tears with the back of her hand. Yvette took his hand and led him down to the where the car was sitting.

"You can't mean that old French car," he said. "My dad collected those for years! He was as passionate about them as you obviously are. I can't believe this. If you want it, it's yours! I mean that. We'd need to get it hauled up to Cambridge where there's a specialist on Citroens. You must tell me all about this when we're heading home. I'm just finishing up."

After placing all the tools carefully into a box and folding up the cord for the compressor machine, they went down to look at the car. Yvette was still swooning, touching it here and there. "It's a precious art object."

"I'll tell you what, Yvette. While you're in Paris, I'll take care of getting the yellow bug moved—with great care on a trailer—up to the shop where they can get it in as good shape as possible. Shall I have them paint it?"

"Oh, no!" Yvette said. "I love it just this way: old and battered." She smiled. "But it does need new tires."

Thayer led her down to the house and showed her, on the second floor, where his favorite bedroom looked over the water and, opening the windows, the beautiful fresh air poured in and on them. He undressed her, she undressed him, and they made intense love in his favorite bed of nine bedrooms as the ocean breeze cooled off the heat.

They heard a car in the driveway, quickly dressed, pulled the cover of the bed in place, and went downstairs.

"Hello, there. Security guards just checking around. You must be a family member, yes? Recently your mother had a system put in to alert us, so here we are. But since you're not a bunch of thieves, I guess we can go now. Enjoy the rest of the day."

Thayer and Yvette sat in the classic Cape Cod wicker chairs for a while on the screened-in front porch, holding hands and feeling the luxurious pre-summer breeze.

Thayer said, "If life could be like this forever, I'd say I'd reached Nirvana."

Yvette answered, "Well, sweetheart, it isn't going to stay like this because I'll have a child with me most of the time. She speaks no English and will most likely be terrified by the new life here. I hope to get a nanny who can speak French to tend to her so you and I can have a good life together. What do you think?"

"I have faith in you. Ultimate faith. We will work out all the bumps and crevasses between the two of us. I believe finding a nanny will not be that hard, especially with summer so close. What a great job it would be for a young girl wanting to learn English!

Don't you have some fancy things to perform at Newport? Couldn't Chloe be a part of that? What a sensation it'd be for a snobby audience in Newport to be outshined by a five-year-old child." He laughed for a long time.

Yvette reminded him that she had to get the job first and go to the French consulate to start the search for a nanny.

They soaked up the breeze until it became chilly. After they locked the house, Yvette patted her treasured car, Thayer put his granite inside a special cloth, and off they went to Boston.

Chapter 20

The drive home was filled with talk of future plans, why Mahler was important, and what other composers were absolute *musts* for Thayer to get to know.

Since they were starving, they stopped in Little Italy and dined at a lovely home-style, small brick restaurant. Being with Thayer was entirely different than eating out with Kolya. There was no bravado, and things were easy and relaxed. They shared a pizza and reflected on the contrast with their Ritz lobster, which produced great amusement and laughter.

The waiter asked if something was wrong with the pizza, and that made them laugh even more before they apologized to him. Fatigue and hunger had simply overtaken them.

Cheese was hanging between Yvette's mouth and the piece she was holding.

Thayer was amused and pulled the cheese into place, licking his finger.

The two stared at each other with wistful and romantic thoughts. In such a short time, they'd be together every night. In just three days, the beds would be delivered.

"What does your mother think about your move?"

"Well, she'd been wondering why I whistle in the house," he said with a grin.

"What is *whistle?*"

As he tried to show her, they only laughed a lot more, which made whistling impossible.

The waiter passed by and demonstrated a whistle.

"I told her I'd found a place to live, and she was slightly nervous about the neighborhood, but she told me she had faith in whatever I chose. She is dying to see the new place. I told her she can have a tour in a week. She started to show me all the stuff I could take with me. Some of it's very nice, and some we just wouldn't want or need. How long do you think it'll take for the enormous meeting with Chloe and the trip back?"

Yvette turned serious. "I want this to go as smoothly and quickly as possible, but I have no set timeline yet. Maybe a week? It might take more." Taking out some paper and pen from her purse, she wrote down her parents' contact information. "Hold onto this, my love, so we can keep in touch." She grabbed his lovely hands and held them tight.

Back at her apartment, the romance took over.

Yvette asked, "Sex twice in one day?"

"Never enough with my perfect Yvette," Thayer answered. He lay down on the floor and lifted her up. "See how manly I can be? I used to run and do crew at Harvard." He put her down slowly, pulled off her work shirt, and kissed her smooth stomach. Her bra came off. Then the unfastening of the pants, and with a wiggle, all Yvette was wearing were her lace underpants.

"I like this look of lace on you … very sexy indeed. I really love you, Yvette." Thayer undressed quickly, and his erection was already prominent.

They thoroughly enjoyed each other's animal instincts and made the most of it all, shaking their heads afterward in a sexual fog.

It was still Sunday, but there were things to tend to. They parted with deep, loving kisses.

Yvette said, "Do not forget about the yellow tin can—the Deux Chevaux!" She slapped her knee and laughed.

Chapter 21

After seeing Dr. Cohen, Yvette checked the mailbox and found a letter from the convent in Reims. Shuddering, she went up to her apartment and nervously opened the letter, which announced to her that a certain "M. d'Argenes" had dropped by the convent to meet the clever piano prodigy. He seemed to be showing some interest in her future. Mother Superior had told him "things have all been arranged." They were grateful for his interest, but there was no chance for any change in the plan that had been drawn up.

That's all I'd need. That creep … that monster … interrupting an "already complicated situation." She groaned. *I can't believe he had the nerve to find her and try to meet her. The nerve! I can't even imagine the what-ifs about this new information.*

She phoned her mother to discuss the possible complications. Her mother helped to calm her with wisdom and quiet patience, guaranteeing that things would indeed go as they had planned.

Yvette could think about Thayer since dinner had been promised to him tonight at six o'clock. She decided to ruminate over Dr. Cohen's advice and not to be thrown into a tailspin by the letter. Gathering the light dinner ingredients was easy when she was still under Dr. Cohen's spell of reason, thoughtfulness, and calm. He was such a good influence.

Tomorrow was a day of chores to be accomplished: the piano and a nanny for Chloe were the primary items to accomplish. When flashes of the new letter exploded in her brain, her stomach turned over, but she was able to control herself.

There was time to put on Mahler's Sixth before Thayer came. Just four days until she could hear it live and alive! Sitting in her only comfortable chair—with her feet up on the table and glass of Amarone in her hand—it was a pleasant hour. One hour of Mahler Sixth, however, was both too much and too little time to take in what she needed, but she persisted to be sure she listened to the final movement, which was the culmination of the entire piece. She tried to remember what Abe had said about it, but she had been thrown into a detour with the nun's news.

When Thayer arrived, it was a breath of spring air that had walked in. She decided not to bother him with this new irritation. "Hello, darling. How was the day?"

"Well, Yvette, I need you to take a walk with me," he said with a smile. "We're going for a swan boat ride right now."

"A swan boat? How wonderful! I've never done that before. I have walked by those boats a hundred times or more since the ice has melted. Let's go!" Yvette's spirits were uplifted, and the walk down to the Public Garden was easy. Just before they got to the boats, Thayer turned down Newbury Street.

Yvette said, "What? But this isn't the way—"

"We have a little errand to take care of first. Just follow me."

They went to a very fine jewelry store and walked in to a big welcome for Dr. Richardson. He took his prize to the ring section and had her try on a lot of samples.

Yvette was completely confused.

Shortly after that, they walked to the swan boats.

"Thayer, what are you doing? Sizing my finger? What's it all about?"

"You'll find out soon enough, my sweet package." He was smiling again.

It was a lovely evening, especially on the swan boat. Gliding slowly over the pond felt dreamy. No motors or noise to deal with—just men pedaling the boats with their feet.

"Okay, Yvette. Here's what it's all about. Will you marry me when you return from Paris?" Silence. Choking for breath. High anxiety and then ----------

"Absolutely yes!"

Tears flowed, and kisses were exchanged. Other passengers clapped and cheered. The boat captain tooted the horn.

Yvette jumped onto Thayer's lap, rocking the boat, and she wept into Thayer's shoulder. "Oh, my darling man. I will be amazingly happy to spend my whole life with you!"

Somebody happened to have a bottle of red wine in his briefcase. He pulled it out and passed it around. Sharing from the same bottle was simply irrelevant; the entire boat was thrilled for Thayer and Yvette.

As the boat proudly glided around the Boston Public Garden, she thought, *He was preparing a real engagement ring—and that's what the fuss at the store was all about.*

Thayer wanted Yvette to walk up the hill to meet his mother on Mount Vernon Street. She agreed, but she became quiet at the thought of visiting his mother's home.

Lydia Richardson answered the door as Thayer was fiddling with the lock. Yvette thought, *What a handsome woman!* She was gracious and warm to Yvette. Lydia had never met any of Thayer's girlfriends. The house was in perfect order at every level: wallpaper of burgundy and white uneven stripes covered the wall until the white wainscot paneling met the stripes. It was almost shocking, but it was extremely attractive. She took Lydia's hand and said, "This is the most elegant home I've ever seen."

Lydia smiled a deeply grateful smile and responded, "This is the most elegant girl I've ever seen. Where in the world did you meet her, Thayer?"

He replied, "On Newbury Street. She's my prize. She's off to Paris for some family affairs, but when she returns, we plan to get married."

"Married? Thayer, I am in shock. How absolutely marvelous to have a Parisian treasure in the family. Oh, goodness. How soon may I tell your brother and sister?"

"Whenever you want, Mother. I know you all thought I'd never settle down and be a husband to anyone, but when the right person walks into your life, it's pretty obvious what to do. Yvette has been studying at the New England Conservatory with Abe Lipinsky—he lives on the hill somewhere—and she knows her music!"

Yvette sat on the velvet couch and smiled. "Mrs. Richardson, your son is the most pure man I have ever met ... and the kindest as well."

"What wonderful words for a mother to hear. I'm still in shock, but it is a great kind of shock. Oh my!" She ran to the kitchen and returned with a small silver tray, three lovely glasses, and a bottle of white wine. They toasted to the union of Thayer and Yvette.

Yvette wanted to make her own toast to Thayer—the love of her life— and to his mother.

Thayer proposed a toast to his new "landlady."

His mother's eyebrows raised at that news.

The rest of the evening flew by. They had dinner at the Café Florian and tossed ideas back and forth as to how one goes about getting married.

Yvette kept having spurts of feeling too excited, but she would find her stability in having physical contact with Thayer.

Thayer kept up his endearing smile.

More talk went on about what chores Yvette had to do before Sunday, when they would see each other between now and then, and what she should bring from Paris for legal purposes for the wedding.

After dinner, they walked back to Yvette's place with their arms intertwined.

Thayer entered with her, and when he saw the letter from France, he asked Yvette what it was about.

She said, "Horrible Jacques is trying to make contact with Chloe."

Thayer said, "No one can legally dispute a will … it named you the sole provider and caretaker of the little girl. How can I help you relax and see things in a better light?"

"I am simply too excited tonight to think of physical acrobatics or even lovemaking."

Thayer left early, and Yvette promised that she'd see the delivery of the beds tomorrow so they could spend the night together on Saint Botolph Street! She decided to keep the engagement a secret from her family until she got to Paris. Life was so exciting!

At nine o'clock, Yvette was the first in line to buy the piano she'd tried out. The payment and delivery were arranged without much complication. She put up signs all over the conservatory and the French Consulate: "Nanny Wanted for Five-Year-Old Child. Must Speak French and Be Willing to Learn or Know English." They recommended other venues to advertise in. Racing around Boston to various schools and colleges took a lot of energy, but she hoped it would bring the results she needed.

The must-do list was shortening. It was nearing the afternoon, and she felt more than ready to take a nap.

Yvette's nap was interrupted and she suddenly sat bolt upright in bed: "'Verklarte Nacht'! Of course. It is totally about Thayer and me!" Her focus shifted from dwelling on Mahler to thinking about the Schoenberg gem. She rummaged around in her papers and found the program notes from months ago. She could prepare Thayer for her latest discovery. Why had she not thought of this before? Educating Thayer not so much about Mahler now. It was about the gorgeous music and story of the couple walking in the night. In the poem by Richard Dehmel, the woman confesses to her new lover that the child she is carrying is not his—but by another man whom she doesn't love. The new lover responds that he will accept this child as his own. Chloe, Thayer, Yvette, the acceptance by Thayer of Chloe's existence, and the care of raising her as his own seemed almost impossibly close to Schoenberg's "Verklarte Nacht."

Chapter 22

❦ ∾ ∾ ∾ ❦

The beds would be delivered soon, and Yvette had no distractions from the official chores of preparing for her trip. The piano would be in the condo on Friday. The beds would be there for tonight's sleep. She'd posted as many signs as she could think of and went to the consulate to have them publish the ad in whatever publication they sent to France.

Calling Pat was slightly embarrassing since she hadn't seen him since she was a wreck at the restaurant with Kolya. She decided to be friendly and tell him her latest news. That would make things seem right.

Pat helped her move her personal items from her bathroom and bedroom to the new home. He arrived in his usual cheerful mood. "I'm happy to see you in such good shape."

When they arrived at Saint Botolph Street, Pat was impressed with her new quarters. Yvette showed him the elegant brass nameplate, and Pat insisted on installing it. Just as they were unloading the last items from the old apartment, the deliverymen arrived. Pat thanked her for her generous tip and took off. Yvette pointed to where each bed should go and had an upsurge of thrilling sensations when she thought of how life was going to be quite different in this lovely place with her lovely man.

It was time to make up the beds and distribute her personal things to the proper places so the bathroom would look lived in and the entire home would be even more welcoming. She shifted a few pieces of furniture around, put her glasses and espresso cups in view, and put out the sheets. (Pat had taken her to a big department store to purchase new blankets.)

By dinnertime, the beds looked homey and inviting with the down comforters in deep blue, spread smoothly over their bed. Yvette lay down to feel the bed. She was asleep in a minute—only to be awakened in half an hour by her buzzer. She went to the intercom, expecting Thayer. Instead, it was Sophie. Yvette didn't want to be bothered by Sophie's confession of her escapade with Kolya and pretended she was too busy to let her in.

Some minutes later, Thayer rang the buzzer. "Well, how great to see your name right out here! Will you let me in?" Thayer strode in in his elegant manner, picked up Yvette, kissed her, and went to look at their bedroom. He was "absolutely taken" by what she had done so quickly.

Hand in hand, they wandered again through their new home and looked at all the furniture in the bedrooms. Only when they passed by Chloe's room did Yvette feel any inner turmoil.

As she showered, she remembered that she had forgotten to pick up the mail. She put on clean clothes so they could walk over to the old apartment and maybe get dinner afterward.

Thayer said, "Are you sure you don't want me to drive over there?"

"I'd love it, but you'll never find a parking space when we get back. Parking is going to be a challenge here, especially with my Deux Chevaux." She grinned broadly. "I'm looking into finding a garage space close by."

"Make that a search for two cars, Yvette. Don't forget that I'll be here too." With that, he tickled her under her arms. "Are you comfortable with me living here while you're away?"

She answered, "Despite my position as your landlady, it is now as much yours as it is mine." She grinned and ran her hand down his face.

They drove over to the old place, and Yvette found two letters in her mailbox. With a gulp, she opened the one from France.

The nuns were informing her that the professor had been looking for Chloe and was threatening to take legal action if he wasn't allowed to see her. The nuns promised to protect the child from anyone but the mother.

Yvette groaned, doubled over, and sat on the stairs next to the elevator—just as Kolya was stepping out of it.

He nodded at her and opened the door. "Sophie has been accepted into the student orchestra at Tanglewood."

Yvette said, "Great. Now you will have two girls with you this summer."

Thayer came inside, double-parked, and told Yvette to bring her mail to the car.

They discussed the implications of Jacques looking into legal action.

Thayer reassured Yvette that it would be "highly unlikely" that anything would come of this.

They parked at the Ritz and had a quiet dinner in the café dining room, the more modest of the eating places. During dinner, Yvette opened her second letter. She was happily surprised to read that they were expecting her at RISD in June to teach her "Great Music" course three days a week.

Yvette remained very quiet with two new pieces of information: Sophie and Tanglewood, Jacques and the convent. She asked Thayer if she could order a martini.

He suggested they stick with wine. "Yvette, I have a little surprise for you." He handed her a small light brown leather box.

When she opened it, she became light headed. Four emerald-cut diamonds were embedded in gold and sparkled like the nighttime stars. Her very own engagement ring! Now she had something gorgeous to focus on. She went over to Thayer, took his face in her hands, and kissed him intensely.

The waiter came over to ask if things were okay, and Yvette answered, "They've never been better!" She then asked Thayer to put it on her finger. It looked absolutely beautiful and outshone all the bad news from just an hour ago. "But I don't have anything for you, my beloved man."

"Only a new and lovely place to live and the promise that you will be with me forever. My darling girl, you have brought joy and beauty and music into my life. How could I ask for anything more?"

Thayer found a decent parking spot for their first night together in their home. Yvette's face was in pain from smiling for so long.

With a welcoming bed, there were no decisions to make. Yvette undressed to her lace underwear and slid into the clean, white sheets.

Thayer got into the other side and quickly put his hands all over Yvette's young body. She laughed lightly at the situation, which wasn't totally conducive to wild sex. *But that's not what I want anymore.* Rolling over to her side, she teased him into putting his lower body next to her backside.

He was now lightly turned on. "This feels too serious," Thayer whispered. "A brand-new bed in a brand-new home. How can we spice up the atmosphere?"

Yvette stood up on the bed—with her left hand showing off her shining ring—and danced around Thayer's body, smiling and laughing with joy.

He grabbed her, stripped off her underwear, and pulled her legs so she was next to him. "My spicy lady, let's see how you smell tonight." He took over until Yvette wasn't laughing anymore. She was breathing deeply as he kissed and licked her everywhere. She immediately went to his waist and then down from there to massage and caress his genitals. They alternated top and bottom, and things progressed quickly.

Yvette and Thayer were worked up into a sexual frenzy, enjoying every body part, every touch, and every breathless word that happened to be cried out. They carried on until Yvette begged him for *real* sex.

Thayer was in a slightly teasing mood and made her wait until he was ready. Eventually, the couple relaxed into a limp state.

"Thayer, come look out here," Yvette called from the bay window area.

He slid out of bed and joined her—both naked, lights out—to look at the house across the street: the lights were on. They enjoyed the simple act of leaning against each other, arms around waists, and watching people living their lives. The table in the window area fit perfectly and in its elegance waited for them to share coffee in the morning.

"I've decided that my Musical Education for Thayer class will not start with Mahler's Sixth but with a piece that is quite appropriate for us. Now, you are still welcome to join me on Saturday night if you want to saturate yourself with Mahler. You do? Great—but we won't focus on him till I'm back from Paris. For now, there is a piece of music that the symphony played when I first arrived. It was thrilling. I knew it from my own experience in Paris, but I never guessed I'd have a chance to hear it live. I will tell you the poem it is based on, and then I'll play the CD for you."

They walked around naked, and Yvette recited the poem. She climbed in his lap, and they listened to the piece.

He told her he was quite overwhelmed with the music. "It is easier to listen to than Mahler, but it is also more difficult."

They kissed and listened to "Verklarte Nacht" again.

He told her that he was more than willing to accept Chloe as his own and hoped to someday have children with Yvette. "This piece is indeed most appropriate," he said.

She handed him an unopened copy of the CD and said he could enjoy it while she was away.

The night was filled with sweet dreams.

Chapter 23

Determined to look her very best for the Mahler event, Yvette picked through her wardrobe. It seemed smaller than when she'd first arrived four months earlier. She managed to put together a decent outfit of multicolored silk pants and a deep red blouse.

Walking to Symphony Hall was simple from Saint Botolph Street. It was almost next door. The cloudy day seemed appropriate for Mahler's Sixth. Tickets in hand, she arrived at the hall in time to find her seat and look around the audience. She saw Monsieur Durup with Philippe! Warm embraces went around, and there were many questions about Philippe and Providence. After a few more steps toward her balcony seat, she ran into Sophie.

Sophie noticed Yvette's ring and gave the expected and appropriate response.

"Have you seen Philippe?" Yvette asked, wondering if Kolya or her French painter was now Sophie's favored boyfriend.

"Oh, he's staying with me. He wondered where you'd disappeared to, but I can see from this amazing ring that you're spending time with your doctor. Are you living in that lovely condo?"

Philippe, with his arm around Sophie's waist, said, "I hear from everyone that this is *the* concert to attend!"

The hall was filling up and feeling too crowded for Yvette's mood.

Yvette assured Philippe that he would be glad he came and abruptly went to the balcony. *Nerves on edge,* she thought, *are natural considering the history right here.*

A thunderbolt awaited in her seat: Kolya was sitting in it. "Yvette, I had to see you before this started. Never forget that I loved you then—and I love you now."

"Kolya, you'd better get down on the stage. By the way, whatever happened to Natalie?"

He said, "We are looking for a nice place to live. She is fragile but mostly fine."

Yvette was relieved, but she didn't understand why. Maybe making him unavailable was the relief.

He whirled out of the seat and leaped toward the stage.

Yvette let out a long, release-filled sigh.

To be sure, Kolya has the energy of a frisky bear. That is the most obvious difference between Thayer and Kolya. But comparisons aren't appropriate because I have the man who was made for me—and I love him in a different way than I ever loved Kolya—but I will never forget my first real love affair. Thoughts went streaming through her mind as she awaited the conductor's appearance onstage.

Ozawa appeared to a loud, responsive audience that was obviously ready for the BSO's final concert of the year. The opening was paced in a way that completely absorbed Yvette's thoughts, feelings, and questions. It was just right! Thrilling, in fact.

Ozawa chose to take the slow movement second, which annoyed Yvette. She preferred the first and second movements to be one arching structure of complexities that were relieved by the balm of the slow third movement. Anyway, Mahler had switched the movements around, even while writing it, and it had gone perfectly. Kolya kept looking up at Yvette. She averted her eyes throughout.

At the end of the large-scale piece—no intermissions seemed the right decision by whoever made such choices—Yvette went to the wine bar and saw Monsieur Durup. They enjoyed dissecting the performance and sipping red wine. Hoping not to see anyone else she knew made their conversation focused and intense. The successful musical afternoon made Yvette feel no hunger at all. Mahler was a first-rate entire meal.

Back at Saint Botolph Street, Yvette ruminated over the afternoon: the music, flashed visions of other friends, and frightening back flashes of Jacques d'Argenes.

"Yvette, you look great!" Thayer said when he made it home. "How did the Mahler go?"

Yvette said, "It was perfect."

"Then why aren't you hanging from the ceiling?"

"It wasn't ceiling-hanging music. It was deeply soul-searching music ... a complete experience."

Thayer picked her up and twirled her around, and her mood immediately switched to a livelier state.

They went out to dinner and chatted about Thayer's day.

"I thought we might go down to Buzzards Bay before tomorrow's concert. What do you think, my darling girl?"

Yvette was ready to jump in the car right then to go to her oasis. She could, once again, see her special Citroen. Now she had two wonderful activities to look forward to tomorrow: Buzzards Bay and Symphony with Thayer.

They packed up the thermos and carefully selected deli foods for the trip. What a surprise it was when they arrived at Cannon Cottage and saw Thayer's brother and nephew. The five-year-old boy was darling and funny. Charley, Thayer's brother, was as jovial as could be. He was overjoyed by this coincidence, which gave him a chance to meet the now-famous Yvette.

They all sat at the kitchen table, ignoring the year's worth of dust, and shared the food. Charley's son, Lowell, kept thanking them for bringing something to eat. He eyed Yvette often and had so many questions for her.

She was taken aback to be with a child who was the same age as Chloe. It almost put her into a slippery zone. Holding Thayer's hand helped her keep her footing. They all went down to the beach, took a pleasant walk, and discussed how to maintain the enormous home. Who would be in charge if they did? What about Celia in Santa Fe? Was she interested in such a family endeavor?

Eventually, Thayer announced that he had a piece of granite waiting for him in the barn.

Yvette needed a swim, and Charley and Lowell had some serious sand castles to build. They all spread out in different directions.

When Charley and Lowell took off in their new BMW, Yvette sat on the porch and felt the pre-summer breeze. She was dreading her trip to Paris. Tears fell slowly down her face, but when Thayer joined her, she managed to seem cheerful. They held hands on the porch until it was time to leave.

Saturday night at Symphony Hall felt too familiar to Yvette, but it was Thayer's first time there. He stared at the beautiful artistry in the old building and noted that the chandeliers. How high up they were! Beethoven's name was inscribed over the stage in huge letters—surrounded by other famous composers' names in slightly smaller letters. There was gold everywhere and red-velvet accents on the railings and seats.

Yvette felt like a pro and introduced her love to the place she loved so intensely. Having buoyed herself up on the beach, she was ready for another fulfillment through Mahler.

The two seats she had bought were under Ozawa's feet. Thayer found his conducting style "enchanting." He was a great student and paid close attention all the way through the hour-plus piece. At the end, he told Yvette that he couldn't stand up to applaud. He was in a musical "state."

When Yvette stood up, she spotted Sophie and Sarah. They were seated far apart. When she looked at Kolya, he was staring at her. Sitting down and still clapping for a great performance, she leaned against Thayer, basking in the aftereffects of such a piece in such a hall next to such a love.

Yvette was torn between having a drink at the bar and taking Thayer to the café where her group gathered. Deciding to keep Mahler at the core, they went to the bar at Symphony Hall, drank champagne, and toasted Thayer's first great musical experience.

Yvette made sure her ring was sparkling and visible … just in case.

They walked home slowly in the drizzle. Once at home, Yvette undressed and told Thayer she was ready for really passionate lovemaking. The night progressed in a most emotional and physical manner.

Morning came all too soon. The suitcase was packed—as it had been for two weeks—and Yvette's plane tickets were in her red leather purse.

Thayer surprised her again. He'd gone to the store on Newbury Street and bought her a beautiful spring suit.

He said, "I want you to arrive in Paris looking up to date."

What a dream he is!

Heading to the airport, dressed in her new outfit, Yvette was silent. She thought about arriving in Boston in the blizzard, the whirlwind of activity with Kolya, Thayer, Chloe, Abe, a job, and music. What was going to become the biggest transfiguration and the deepest force in her life? And would Jacques be waiting for her in Paris to ruin everything?

149